"You!" they both s doing here at C

Dale grinned. "I work here."

At the same time, Petra said, "I live here. My aunts invited me to stay until the hotel is finished."

"You're a Chatam!" Dale declared.

"Petra Chatam," she confirmed, comprehension dawning in her warm amber eyes.

"I should've known." He reached out to tap the delicate cleft in her dainty chin, but at the last moment, stopped himself. "That and the eyes. Though, yours are darker, which is odd because your hair is so..." *Beautiful*, he thought.

"It's good of you to inspect the job that your crew is doing on the new suite."

"Uh, I *am* the crew," he informed her.

She blinked at that, and he could almost see himself coming down in her estimation, from partner and project manager to lowly carpenter. Uncharacteristically, his temper spiked. He was proud of what he did.

But he didn't kid himself that he lived on the same plain as Garth Anderton. Or the Chatams.

But he was shocked to find that it suddenly mattered....

Books by Arlene James

Love Inspired

ARLENE JAMES

says, "Camp meetings, mission work and church attendance permeate my Oklahoma childhood memories. It was a golden time, which sustains me yet. However, only as a young widowed mother did I truly begin growing in my personal relationship with the Lord. Through adversity He has blessed me in countless ways, one of which is a second marriage so loving and romantic it still feels like courtship!"

After thirty-three years in Texas, Arlene James now resides in Bella Vista, Arkansas, with her beloved husband. Even after seventy-five novels, her need to write is greater than ever, a fact that frankly amazes her, as she's been at it since the eighth grade. She loves to hear from readers, and can be reached via her website, www.arlenejames.com.

Building a Perfect Match

Arlene James

Love Inspired

Recycling programs for this product may not exist in your area.

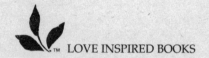

LOVE INSPIRED BOOKS

ISBN-13: 978-0-373-87740-9

BUILDING A PERFECT MATCH

www.LoveInspiredBooks.com

Printed in U.S.A.

Charm is deceptive, and beauty is fleeting;
but a woman who fears the LORD is to be praised.
Honor her for all that her hands have done, and
let her works bring her praise at the city gate.
— *Proverbs* 31:30–31

Some daughters-in-law are sweet and thoughtful. Some are brilliant and talented. Some are beautiful and fun. Some are industrious and hardworking. Some are good wives, and some are good moms. Some are dedicated Christian women.

I hit the jackpot and got all of the above!

This one's for you, Monica.

MomR

Chapter One

"Well, sis," Asher Chatam said, smiling across his desk at Petra, "you're bringing the old Vail Hotel back to life. How does it feel?"

"The Anderton Vail," Garth Anderton, CEO of Anderton Hotels, corrected, passing a stack of papers to the man on his right.

Petra flashed a careful smile at her older brother, who, as the attorney for Bowen & Bowen Construction, had drawn up the contracts now being signed for the renovation of the historic hotel. Knowing well her reputation among the members of her own family, she silently prayed for success.

Lord, this is my chance to achieve something, to finally find my place in the world. Please help me pull this off.

At twenty-eight, Petra had flitted from one "career" to another, never quite finding her calling, her passion, while her siblings, high achievers all, had long ago settled into their chosen fields. Now, as Special Assistant to the CEO of Anderton Hotels, she finally had an opportunity to do something meaningful—right here in Buffalo Creek, Texas, the hometown of her parents, both physicians who resided in Waco, where she had grown up.

She had brought the Vail to the attention of Garth Anderton soon after going to work for his company. Garth, who had built the Anderton chain by renovating small, historic hotels in good locations into unique and profitable properties, had been skeptical at first, as Buffalo Creek lay nearly forty miles to the south of the downtown centers of both Dallas and Fort Worth. The value of the property, however, along with the cost-plus contract that Petra had negotiated with Bowen & Bowen, had convinced Anderton of the viability of the project.

Now, if Petra could just bring this off on budget and schedule, she stood to be named manager of the hotel. Then, Garth had promised, after a few months he would bring her on to the acquisitions team. She would be perfectly placed, and on a career trajectory at last, when he took the company international.

Yet so much could go wrong. Her business degree hadn't exactly prepared her for overseeing the renovations of a historic hotel, let alone managing it. Plus, Garth himself presented something of a problem. Twice divorced, he had a reputation for dating and marrying his employees. Though he constantly cast out lures, Petra was determined not to bite. It meant walking a tightrope on the job, never taking up Garth on his more personal suggestions and constantly doing her best work.

Walton Bowen, the senior partner at the construction company, finished signing the papers and laid aside his ink pen. A big man with graying brown hair and smiling hazel eyes, he rose to his feet and shook hands all around before leaving the office. Petra and Garth followed a few moments later, strolling along the square to the southeast corner in the ninety-plus-degree heat. They crossed the street to the Vail and pushed through the bronze-and-glass doors.

Petra did not recall a time when the hotel had been operational. During her many visits to see her aunties in Buffalo Creek, the old hotel had stood silent and empty, the peach-colored marble columns and grand staircase rising in ghostly splendor behind the thick glass of its murky windows. As a child, Petra had often stood with her nose pressed to the glass, imagining those who had climbed the steps and moved through the lobby.

Though the major contracts had just been signed, work had already begun on the first phase of the project, which involved Garth's personal quarters. The new construction had left the soaring lobby looking more like a war zone than a luxury hotel in the making, however. Dust coated everything in sight, from the dull but intricately carved registration desk to the gapped crystal chandeliers overhead.

Suddenly dismayed, Petra scrunched her toes inside her shoes. It didn't help that her spectator pumps, which perfectly complemented her paper-white linen suit and black, sleeveless turtleneck, had turned out to be nothing more than attractive vises to torture her feet. Picking her way through the debris littering the marble floor, she wished mightily that she'd worn sensible flats.

"We've got quite a job cut out for us," Garth Anderton decreed, nodding his frosty head.

"Still," she said determinedly, "the beauty is here. Just look at that." She pointed toward the scrolls beneath the pediment of the nearest column.

"Of course, it's not real gold leaf," Garth pronounced, tilting back to eye the rich metallic glow far overhead.

"Oh, but it is," said a new voice. Firm and masculine, that voice carried the weight of knowledge.

Petra turned her dark amber gaze toward the sound, her blond ponytail swishing between her shoulder blades. The speaker stood in the doorway of one of the inner offices. Easily one of the best-looking men she'd ever seen, present company included, he stood at least an inch or two over six feet. Like Garth, he seemed exceptionally fit, but the tool belt slung about his slim hips proved that the muscles bulging in his upper chest and forearms came as the result of hard labor, while Garth's slender physique was owed entirely to the workout routine designed by his personal trainer. Other differences stood out starkly.

Casually dressed in jeans, boots and a yellow T-shirt that brought out the vibrant green of his eyes, the stranger obviously depended less on packaging than Garth, who prided himself on his grooming and wardrobe. At thirty-nine, Garth appeared several years the elder, but his frosty blond hair had been cut and styled to reflect the latest trend, while the longer, gold-streaked bronze locks of the interloper appeared somewhat unkempt. Yet not even the shadow of a morning beard dimmed the impact of that wryly smiling face, with its deeply set eyes, and lean cheeks grooved with dimples. In short, Petra found this unfamiliar man disturbingly attractive—and to her horror, everyone seemed to know it!

Garth's dark eyes narrowed behind the rectangular frames of glasses the exact shade of silvery gray as his summer-weight Italian suit. "I beg your pardon?" he intoned, his voice cold enough to leave icicles on the newcomer's perfect nose.

"The gold leaf on the capitals," said the other man easily, his vibrant green gaze on Petra as he walked across the floor to place a hand on one of the smooth columns. He smiled and nodded before addressing Garth again. "It's real. Which is why it was scraped off the bases."

Garth folded his arms, a sure sign of irritation, but then he quickly stepped forward to offer a perfectly manicured hand. "Garth Anderton, and you are?"

"Dale Bowen."

So this was the other half of Bowen & Bowen Construction, Walton Bowen's son. Petra silently thanked God that she hadn't had to deal with him during the contract negotiations; her discussions with his father had been tense enough, and he did not set her on edge the way the younger Bowen did. Torn between fleeing for cover and basking in that openly interested green gaze, she just stood there staring mutely. When he clapped palms with Garth and switched his attention there, she felt a spurt of relief.

The two men measured each other with blunt, level looks. Finally, Garth put on his easy, gleaming white smile, the one meant to disarm.

He knew as well as she did that Dale Bowen was a partner in the construction firm to which they were now legally bound, but he had to try to take the guy down a peg by saying, "You must be the project manager."

"I am," Bowen said, sounding amused.

Petra cleared her throat in warning to Garth. Clearly, here was one "construction type," as Garth would say, who wouldn't be easily intimidated. Garth took the throat clearing as a bid for introduction and waved her forward with a frown.

"My Special Assistant, Petra."

"Pleased to meet you," Bowen said, and once again she felt the full impact of that green gaze. He shook her hand, his own much larger one emanating bone-melting heat. The man was human lava. Garth, by comparison, always managed to be as cool as a cucumber. Petra suddenly wanted to cuddle up to Bowen. Instead, she yanked her hand back.

"Well, Dale," Garth said, purposefully using the other man's given name, "I'm sure you agree that we should consider a less costly alternative to real gold leaf." He looked up at the gold gleaming far overhead, and so missed the shake of Dale Bowen's head. "How difficult will it be to match the color?"

"Not very," Bowen answered, "but it doesn't matter. Use anything other than original materials anytime they're available and the BCHS will be all over you."

Garth settled a frown on the other man. "BCHS?"

"That would be the Buffalo Creek Historical Society," Petra volunteered.

"It would," Bowen confirmed, smiling at her before switching his gaze back to her boss. "I've worked hand-in-hand with them for years, and I'm warning you now. Use the wrong materials or methods such as pre-hung doors, and they'll go to the state to shut you down."

"But the security of our guests—"

"Won't be compromised in the least if we reuse the original doors," Bowen interrupted.

"What about cost?" Garth demanded.

"Probably about the same. The real issue is the time it'll take to strip and refinish."

"Time, as I'm sure you know," Garth growled, "is money."

Bowen looked him in the eye, his sculpted mouth curving in a tight smile. Petra noticed that the square tip of his chin flattened when he smiled. Her own somewhat pointed chin had a tiny cleft in it, a Chatam family trait, and it tended to disappear when she smiled.

"Trust me," he said, "reusing the original hardwood doors will take less time and money than fighting the BCHS."

"We'll see about that," Garth muttered. Turning to Petra, he ordered, "Do a cost analysis."

"Yes, sir." She nodded, carefully avoiding Bowen's gaze.

"I want to see my private apartment now," he barked at Bowen. With that, he headed for the staircase. Petra trailed after him on her aching feet.

Behind them, Bowen asked dryly, "Wouldn't you prefer to use the elevator?"

Garth stopped so suddenly that Petra bumped into him from behind. Turning on his heel, he glared at the construction manager over the top of her head. "Fine."

Petra closed her eyes in relief. The thought of climbing five flights of stairs to the roof in these shoes made her want to weep. Garth didn't seem as pleased. Grasping her by the elbow, he grimly marched her toward the elevator tucked into a corner at the end of the reception area. Dale Bowen fell in beside her as they drew up in front of the outer doors of the elevator. Constructed of glass inlaid with bronze, the doors showed the polished wood interior of the waiting elevator car. Bowen pushed a button and the glass doors slid open. The trio walked into the elevator and turned to face the front. Dale took a key from his pocket and inserted it into a lock in the control panel. When he turned it, the doors slid closed.

"You can take them off now," he said as the elevator slowly lifted away from the ground floor.

"What?" Garth snapped.

Bowen ignored him, dropping his leaf-green gaze on Petra instead. "You can take off your shoes now," he said gently. "The floors in the penthouse are clean."

"Oh." Surprised, she looked down at her feet. "How did you…" She broke off, wincing with embarrassment. And she'd thought no one had noticed. Garth certainly hadn't!

"My mom and sister like pretty shoes, too," Bowen told her with a knowing smile. "They call them 'cruel shoes' because they can't resist buying them even though they hurt when they wear them."

Garth finally realized what Dale Bowen had obviously surmised with a glance. Not to be outdone, he slipped an arm about Petra's shoulders. "By all means," he cooed solicitously, "take off your shoes if they're uncomfortable."

The intimacy of his tone and gesture heightened Petra's embarrassment. Quickly stepping out of the shoes, she stooped to pick them up by the heels. Thankfully, the elevator came to a stop just then, and the door slid open.

"Well, well," Garth said, sounding pleasantly surprised.

"This way," Bowen directed, lifting a hand and sliding past Petra to push open the tall, carved doors that stood across a narrow length of gleaming wood floor.

Petra gasped as she stepped into the private apartment. Twelve-foot-high ceilings radiated with hidden lights, augmenting the sunshine that spilled through the broad windows set deeply into the paneled walls. French doors in one end of the living area overlooked an enclosed patio. Black granite and steel appliances accented the small, well-appointed kitchen, separated by a bar from the greater room. The two bedrooms, each with a private bath, opened off a short hallway.

As was his practice with every hotel added to the Anderton chain, Garth had contracted the apartment separately and given his personal decorator, Dexter, control of this portion of the overall project. Dexter had done well.

"Excellent," Garth said, brushing back the sides of his suit coat with both hands. "At least the historical society didn't hold up things on this end."

"This falls under the heading of new construction," Bowen pointed out.

"Excellent," Garth said again, looking around. "Quality work."

"And on budget," Bowen added. The sound of a revving engine had him reaching for his pocket, from which he pulled a cell phone. "Excuse me." Crossing the room, he tapped the tiny screen and lifted the phone to his ear. "This is Dale."

Petra turned away, affording him as much privacy as possible, and found Garth watching her. He stepped close enough to lightly brush a hand down her arm.

"Pretty nice, huh?"

"Lovely," she agreed, shifting away.

"And roomy," he went on, adding softly. "You know, staying here would be much more convenient for you than that old family mausoleum across town."

Petra kept a smile firmly in place as she whispered, "Chatam House is blocks, not miles, away and my aunts would be offended if I didn't stay with them." Triplets in their seventies, the sisters held some old-fashioned but laudable ideas about hospitality and family.

"Just tell them you need to be on-site," Garth pressed.

"If I stay anywhere else," Petra insisted quietly, "their feelings will be hurt. Besides, Chatam House isn't a mausoleum. It's quite grand, actually."

Garth narrowed his eyes. "I'd like to see that for myself."

"I'll have my aunts issue an invitation when it's convenient," she returned lightly. "You understand, of course, that it's a busy time for them just now."

Her Aunt Odelia was getting married after more than seventy years of maidenhood—to the same man she'd jilted fifty years earlier! Petra's brother, Asher, had also married last month, and two family weddings in so short a space of time had had the house in an uproar for weeks. The former gardener, Garrett Willows, had recently married, too, so of course the aunties had insisted on hosting a small reception for him and his bride. No, this was not an optimal time to introduce a new face into the mix, and Petra could only be glad of that. She was having enough difficulty keeping this relationship on a business footing as it was.

Bowen returned. "Sorry. I've been trying to track down—" He broke off. "Never mind. Another job. Now then, if you've finished here, we need to stop on the third floor to take a look at a problem with the railings there."

"What problem?" Garth asked, frowning.

"They're gone," Bowen reported. "Whole sections of them. And none of my suppliers can find anything like them. We're probably looking at having them replicated."

Garth threw up his hands and charged for the door. "I don't suppose we could just replace them with something similar?"

"We're not going to find anything similar," Bowen called out to him, following. He stopped and held the door open for

Petra, who hurried through on her bare feet. He winked, as if to say that the boss was having a bad day.

Petra had the sinking feeling that it was only going to get worse, and she proved entirely correct.

The two men disagreed on everything from the depth of the carpet pile to the placement of light switches. Petra thought Garth would pop a blood vessel when it came to the issue of closets, of all things. The Vail didn't have any, and Dale doubted that the historical society would approve of having them built.

Garth finally turned on his heel and stormed off. Petra shot Dale Bowen an apologetic glance before hurrying after Garth in her killer shoes. This project was becoming more complicated by the moment, and she couldn't help worrying.

Please, Lord, she prayed, *please help me work it all out. For once, Lord, help me get it right!*

Bam! The pickup truck rocked as Dale slammed the door. He took a firm grip on the steering wheel with both hands and closed his eyes, calming himself.

Okay, Lord, he thought, *it's obvious this job isn't going to be easy.*

"Man," he added aloud, "that guy rubs me the wrong way!"

Sucking air in through his nose, Dale blew it out again through his mouth. An image of Special Assistant Petra popped up in his mind. Average height with a truly lovely face, she had captured his interest instantly. Unfortunately, she was obviously very "special" to Garth Anderton, even though he had to be forty if he was a day, and she couldn't be older than her mid-twenties.

Not that it's any of my business, Dale admitted silently, frowning.

Business. He'd somehow forgotten the importance of this job as soon as he'd laid eyes on the woman, which wasn't like him at all, especially considering that business had been slow these past couple of years and the doctor had told his dad to take it easy. Sitting back in his seat, Dale closed his eyes again and began to pray.

Lord, You know that we need this job. This one job could let Dad step back, maybe even retire, so please give me what it takes to see it through. Amen.

Feeling better, Dale started up his white, double-cab truck and eased it out of the alley and onto the street flanking the downtown square with its turn-of-the-century, pink granite courthouse and circa 1930s storefronts. A few blocks later, he turned right onto Chatam Avenue then made a sharp left.

He'd been guiding his truck through the black wrought iron gate and up the easy slope in the circular drive to the big antebellum mansion—built in 1860—on the hill for weeks now. Soon after Odelia Chatam and Kent Monroe, both in their seventies, had gotten engaged, the Chatam sisters had hired him to reconfigure several rooms into a suite for the newlyweds. Dale had been pleased to take on the job, but with the three sisters' insistence that he not work before nine in the morning or after five in the afternoon, the project had been slow going.

Still, the Chatam sisters were generous Christian women. His buddy Garrett Willows had worked as their gardener after he'd gotten out of prison, and the sisters had allowed Dale to take time away from the Chatam House renovation in order to help Garrett and his new wife open a florist shop and plant nursery in Kent Monroe's old Victorian house. Then they'd helped Garrett get a much-deserved pardon.

Pulling the truck through the porte cochere at the west side of the mansion, Dale parked it out of sight, then gathered his tools and let himself into the back hall through the yellow door. As was his custom, he stopped by the kitchen to elbow open the swinging door and let the cook know he was on the premises.

"Hilda, I'm here."

"Well, that makes two of us, sugar," she quipped, turning from the sink. As wide as she was tall, with lank, straight hair cropped just below her chin, she winked at him. "I'll let the misses know."

"Thanks."

Backing out of the doorway, he continued down the hall to the end, only to turn right into another that flanked the massive marble-and-mahogany staircase, which anchored the foyer at the front of the house. Dale always looked up when he started the climb. He dearly loved the painted ceiling with its ruffled clouds and white feathers against a sunny blue backdrop. No one could tell him who the artist had been, but he'd certainly been a genius.

The grand staircase, with its yellow marble steps and ornately carved mahogany banister, was an architectural wonder that few could appreciate more than the skilled carpenter who crossed the landing and went to work opening a new doorway into the unfinished suite.

Dale managed the chore with a minimum of noise and mess, while wolfing down his lunch, answering numerous phone calls from other jobs and, if he were to be honest, thinking about the blonde whom he'd left back at the hotel. He couldn't help wondering about her. She hadn't worn a ring, so he assumed she was single, but that didn't mean she was unattached. Anderton had made his interest in her clear enough.

That didn't mean they were involved, though.

Neither did it mean that Dale ought to get involved with her himself. He wanted an old-fashioned Christian girl, like his mom, a homemaker who valued family above all else. All he knew about Petra was that he was attracted to her. Maybe he'd get a chance to know her better, and maybe he wouldn't. That was up to God.

Dale nailed the header in place with just enough time remaining in the workday to clean up the site before heading home. He pulled out his phone to call home and let everyone know that he was on his way. With his attention on his phone, he wandered out onto the broad landing toward the stairwell, only to bump into someone coming from the other direction.

"Sorry!"

Looking up, Dale meant to reply to the surprised female voice with an apology for not watching where he was going—and nearly dropped his phone, along with his jaw.

Petra stood on the top step in her bare feet, one slender hand on the curled end of the banister, the other holding her black-and-white shoes by the heels. Her sleek ponytail lay across one shoulder.

For a moment, Dale thought he'd conjured her up from his imagination, but then he backed up a step and watched recognition overtake her. Shock swiftly followed.

He knew just how she felt, especially when she smiled.

Chapter Two

❧

"You!" they both said. "What are you doing here?"

Dale grinned. "I work here," he supplied.

At the same time, she said, "I live here."

They both laughed, and Dale spread his arms, trying to take in the situation. That simple act seemed to kick his brain into gear.

"Did you say that you *live* here?"

"That's right," she answered, nodding. "My aunts invited me to move in until the hotel is finished. Once I'm manager, I'll find my own place."

"You're a Chatam!" Dale declared, smacking himself in the forehead—with his phone, as it turned out.

"Petra Chatam," she confirmed, comprehension dawning in her warm amber eyes. "Ah. Garth didn't say, did he?"

"No. No, he didn't," Dale agreed, feeling ridiculously pleased. "But I should've known."

She raised her slender eyebrows at that. "How on earth could you?"

He reached out to tap the delicate cleft in her dainty chin, but at the last moment thought better of the gesture and reached back to tap his own chin instead. "That and the eyes. Though yours are darker, which is odd because your hair is so…" *Beautiful,* he thought inanely. He managed, belatedly, to say, "Light."

She tilted her head. "You work here?"

He pointed behind him. "On the new suite."

"I see. I didn't realize. Well, it's good of you to inspect the job that your crew is doing."

"Uh, I *am* the crew on this particular job," he informed her.

She blinked at that, and he could almost see himself coming down in her estimation, from partner and project manager to lowly carpenter. Uncharacteristically, his temper spiked. He was proud of what he did, proud of his skills and knowledge, proud to work with his father in a family-owned business, proud to be his own boss and provide jobs for others, proud of the quality of the work provided by Bowen & Bowen Construction. But he didn't kid himself that he lived on the same plain as Garth Anderton. Or the Chatams for that matter.

Shocked to find that it suddenly did matter, he frowned and heard himself say, "Your boss is in for a tough time with the Historical Society."

She parked her hands at her waist, the shoes sticking out in sharp-toed splendor from the fist that gripped them. "Maybe they're in for a tough time with him. It's not like he doesn't have a great deal of experience, you know. He has done this before."

"He hasn't done it in Buffalo Creek."

"True. But I'm sure his experience elsewhere will prompt him to—"

"Make enemies of the Society, most likely," Dale put in testily.

"You don't know that!" she shot back.

"I know his type," Dale snapped. "Used to throwing his weight around and getting what he wants when he wants it."

She bowed her head in an obvious attempt to curb her

own tongue. Dale knew that he'd do well to follow her example, but something about Garth Anderton provoked him even when the guy was not around.

"Look," he said in a softer tone, "I just want to avoid trouble. I know every member of the Society, and they're not going to take kindly to any attempt at cutting corners."

"Anderton doesn't cut corners," she insisted. "It's just that time is of the essence."

"Uh-huh," Dale retorted gracelessly. "I don't think the Society's idea of the importance of time and his are the same thing. They honor times past and seek to preserve for the future what it leaves behind. Anderton's after a quick buck."

"He's a businessman," she argued. "What's wrong with that?"

"Not a thing," he conceded. "I'm a businessman myself, but I know something about historical sites, restoration and those who care about them. Believe me, the only way to save time here is to get it right from the first."

She bit her lip, eyelashes batting. Clearly, she didn't agree but wouldn't argue the point further. Dale wished that he'd bitten his tongue, but the best thing he could do now was beat a hasty retreat before he upset her further.

"I, uh, I have to go. It, um, was nice to meet you. Again."

Wincing inwardly, he twisted past her and pounded down the stairs, mentally kicking himself. Really, could he have been any more confrontational? Any less suave? He pictured Garth Anderton's urbane face and the way he'd so possessively slipped his arm about Petra Chatam's shoulders in the elevator earlier. Suddenly, Dale wanted to pound something else, if only to punish his own fists.

Moving toward her joint bedroom and sitting room with labored steps, Petra winced. That had gone about as well as her choice of footwear. The man had usurped her day from beginning to end. He "irritated" Garth, who had already given her orders to have him removed as the construction supervisor on the project. She'd already made an appointment to speak with Walton Bowen about the matter the next morning. As much as she dreaded the prospect, bumping into Dale right here at Chatam House somehow made it worse. Nevertheless, orders were orders.

Now, if only she could figure out how to go about the thing without offending everyone she knew and loved. Her brother, Asher, had sung the praises of Mr. Bowen the elder and his company. Now it turned out that her aunties had hired Mr. Bowen the younger to make the necessary changes in their beloved mansion. Great. Just great.

What was she supposed to say to the Bowens tomorrow, anyway? That the boss just didn't like Dale? Or maybe that the younger man displayed entirely too much knowledge and confidence in his opinions? She certainly wasn't going to admit that she would be as relieved as Garth to have Dale Bowen out of the way—but for other reasons entirely.

While changing into loose slacks, a knit top and her most comfortable flats, she decided that she would speak to her aunts about the matter. They seemed to know the Bowens. They might be able to advise her how best to approach the situation. Resolved, Petra padded into the well-appointed bedroom to comb her thick, straight hair before appearing downstairs.

As expected, she found her aunties and Kent Monroe in the front parlor, awaiting the dinner hour. Magnolia smiled at her from the armchair placed at a right angle to the settee, where Odelia and Kent cuddled, and the high-backed wing-chair that Hypatia habitually claimed. Hypatia looked around as the others smiled in Petra's direction. Her mood lightening already, Petra smiled back, if only because Odelia sat swathed in layers of peach chiffon, from the big fluffy bow in her white hair to the ruffled toes of what looked suspiciously like bedroom slippers, not that Odelia gave a fig. She wore what she wanted and let the world gawk—and Kent moon. He did so adore her, and that was another reason to smile. The fact that he habitually hauled his great belly onto his feet in gesture of old-world gentility whenever a woman entered the room was yet another.

"Oh, Pet," Odelia trilled, using the nickname that Petra's late grandfather had coined. Odelia waved a lace hanky, jiggling the enormous square rhinestones clipped to her earlobes. They resembled framed, faceted mirrors. "Come and join us."

Magnolia gestured toward another armchair at the end of the rectangular piecrust tea table, sadly lacking a tea tray at the moment. Petra rarely drank the stuff, especially in the summer, but tea was somehow necessary at Chatam House, as much a part of the gracious atmosphere as the antiques and old-world manners. And after the day she'd had, Petra could have used a cup.

"It's so nice to have a young person in the house again," Hypatia decreed, though in truth Garrett, Jessa and their young son Hunter had vacated the premises only a few weeks ago, along with Ellie Monroe, Kent's granddaughter and Petra's new sister-in-law. Dressed for dinner in her customary silk and pearls, her silver hair twisted into its customary chignon, Hypatia inclined her neat head as if she were a queen acknowledging a subject, but the elegant old dear was nothing if not loving and kind.

"How are things going at the hotel?" Magnolia asked. Ever the practical one, she wore her shirtwaist dresses until they were threadbare, augmenting them with odd pieces of her late father's attire and on occasion trading her penny loafers for galoshes. Her steel-gray hair lay upon her slender shoulder in its usual simple braid.

Looking at the three of them, Petra felt her heart swell. She'd always found acceptance and unconditional love here. Not that her own parents, brothers and sisters didn't love her, of course. It was just that she'd somehow never quite measured up to the rest of them.

But she had a chance to *do* something now, a shot at a real career. So long as she didn't blow it.

"I was wondering," she said, taking her seat, "what you could tell me about Dale Bowen."

The sisters traded looks as Kent gingerly lowered himself onto the settee once more.

"He's really very nice," Odelia volunteered, "and so very handsome, don't you think?" She giggled at Kent, who teasingly shook a finger in silent warning.

"He's very competent," Magnolia put in, "very skilled."

"I find him respectful, mannerly and considerate," Hypatia said. "We know his family, of course, from church. Very solid people. What in particular did you wish to know, dear?"

Petra shifted uncomfortably. Maybe this wasn't such a good idea, after all. "I—I'm not sure really. It's just that we *could* be working together on the hotel renovation, and I like to know all I can about the people I work with."

Hypatia nodded her understanding. "Well, he's a dutiful son, a regular at church, steady, dependable. What the man does not know about construction has not been imagined yet, and he treats historical treasures with the reverence that they deserve. I might wish that he were a little less fond of electric saws, but I cannot fault his work ethic, his manners, his attitude—"

"Or his looks," Odelia interjected with another giggle. Kent made a growling sound, purely for show, but Odelia leaned over, placed her hand on his forearm and cooed, "I'm in love, dearest, but I'm not blind."

Chuckling, Kent folded her doughy hand in his and raised it to his lips. "Neither am I, my darling, but I have eyes only for you."

Odelia dissolved in breathless twitters, prompting Magnolia to roll her eyes and rise to her feet.

"I believe I'll see what is holding up dinner," she announced, turning for the door.

"Perhaps we'll just wait in the dining room," Kent said suggestively, hauling himself up again and pulling Odelia with him.

Hypatia watched them leave, arm in arm, before turning to Petra with a weary sigh. "They say the enchantment will wear off eventually, but with those two I'm not so sure."

Petra bit back a smile. "It's the romance of the wedding, I'm sure."

"One can hope," Hypatia muttered. "Now, dear, what were we discussing?"

"Well," Petra hedged, "I was just wondering if Dale Bowen is the right man for the hotel job."

"Undoubtedly," Hypatia decreed.

Deflated, Petra glanced at her lap. "Ah. It's just that he seems spread pretty thin, what with this job and helping out his friends and…everyone has a private life." Everyone but her.

"Oh, I don't think he's seeing anyone just now," Hypatia said off-handedly. "If he were, I'm sure his mother would have told me."

That news sent a little shiver of *something* through Petra. She ruthlessly suppressed it. So what if he was single and unattached? It made no difference to her.

"I'm just concerned that he won't be able to give us his undivided attention," she went on carefully. "At the hotel, that is. We're on a tight schedule, and any delays could mean…" *My job.* "Added difficulty."

"You needn't worry, my dear," Hypatia assured her. "You're in good hands with Dale Bowen."

Smiling wanly, Petra silently conceded defeat. "Nice to know."

"Speaking of getting to know those with whom you work, dear," Hypatia said, "I was wondering about Mr. Anderton."

Petra's gaze sharpened. "Really? Why? What have you heard?" Her aunties were not the sort to read the scandal sheets or indulge in gossip, but something in Hypatia's tone had sent up warning flares.

"Only that he is a very presentable, successful gentleman and unattached, I believe. Your sister mentioned him."

Petra wondered what else Dallas had told them about Garth and why she had bothered. Dallas was known to meddle and blithely took credit for getting Odelia and Kent back together after a half-century-long separation. She fancied herself something of a matchmaker, but she knew that Petra was focused on establishing herself in her career and uninterested in romance. Still, the fact that Dallas had bothered to even check out Garth annoyed Petra almost as much as Garth's agitating for an introduction to her family. She suspected that he meant to charm them out of any objections they might have to his pursuit of her, and that made the fine hairs stand up on the back of her neck.

She shook away the sensation and found Hypatia studying her with gentle concern.

"Is something wrong, dear?"

"No, no."

Odelia rushed back into the room just then, Kent lumbering in her wake. "Sister!" she cried. "The violinist we hired for the reception has broken his arm! Whatever will we do?"

Hypatia twisted in her chair. "Oh, dear. Well, perhaps the twins—"

"They're playing for the ceremony!" Odelia exclaimed. "Not the reception!"

"We'll think of something," Hypatia said, pinching the bridge of her nose. Petra took that as her cue to leave.

"If you'll excuse me, I'd like to wash my hands before dinner."

"Of course," Hypatia said absently.

Petra all but ran. The last thing she wanted was to get

caught up in the wedding fever. She was happy for Aunt Odelia and Kent, but she couldn't let anything sidetrack her just now, especially not a man.

Pausing at the head of the stairs, Hypatia caught the faint sounds of a television program. She looked to her left, noting the narrow band of light that shined beneath the door to the combination bedroom and sitting room that Petra had taken for her own. She'd said she'd be looking for her own space once the renovations on the hotel were completed. All three of the sisters had hurried to assure her that she was welcome to stay at Chatam House as long as she liked, even permanently, but Hypatia suspected that Petra wasn't really thinking that far ahead.

Concerned for some time now about her sweet niece, Hypatia started toward Petra's door, but then she paused, wondering if an old woman's company was what Petra needed. Sadly, Hypatia was not really sure what her niece needed. Petra had always seemed a little lost somehow. The girl was perfectly capable, of course. She'd held a number of interesting jobs since graduating from college, but she'd never seemed to settle into anything, and so far as Hypatia knew, she hadn't dated much, either.

Hypatia could identify. She hadn't been much interested in dating herself, not in her youth and certainly not now. So much of the world seemed intent on pairing off, but she had never seen the point of it all. Then again, she'd always had her sisters. Triplets shared an incredible bond. It seemed almost unthinkable that one of them should marry, especially at this stage of life! Hypatia had always assumed that one must be called to marriage as one was called to ministry. Yet here was Odelia about to marry at the very end of her life—or nearly so.

Odelia Monroe. The notion still boggled the mind.

Hypatia considered another niece, Petra's younger sister,

Dallas. While Petra seemed to avoid more than the most casual of relationships with men, Dallas dated frequently, throwing over one fellow after another in her search for *Mr. Perfect,* having declared early on that *Mr. Right* simply wasn't good enough!

Neither girl seemed to have a clue about true romance or God's calling in her life.

And yet, Petra had asked about Dale Bowen. Hypatia sensed that something more than professional concern lay beneath those seemingly casual queries. Could it be romantic interest?

Sighing, she had to admit that Chatam House had somehow become Romance Central. It had all started with their nephew, Reeves, and the granddaughter, Anna, of their good friend, Tansy Burdett. Then their niece Kaylie had met her husband, Stephen, when he'd come to Chatam House to recover from an accident. After that, it had been Kaylie's brother Chandler and Bethany, the sister of their former gardener, Garrett Willows, who, as it happened, had met and married his wife, Jessa, at Chatam House just last month. Oh, and one mustn't forget Asher, Petra's brother and another nephew, and Ellie, Kent's granddaughter. Their romance had paralleled Kent and Odelia's.

Chatam House hadn't seen so many happy couples since… well, ever! Perhaps it had to do with the upcoming wedding. Once that was behind them, surely things would get back to normal.

Hypatia laughed at herself. As if anything would ever be "normal" again after Odelia married. Well, they'd just have to find a *new* normal. God would show them the way. It wasn't as if Odelia was leaving them, after all. They were gaining a brother, not losing a sister. They had all discussed it, she and her sisters.

Who discussed such things with Petra? Hypatia wondered. She and Dallas loved each other, but they didn't seem that close, and their mother, Maryanne, had always been so busy with her practice. Troubled, Hypatia moved to the door of Petra's room and lightly knocked.

Petra called for her to enter, and she did so, slipping quietly into the comfortable room. "I just thought I'd check on you, dear," she explained. "You seemed...preoccupied at dinner."

Pointing the remote at the flat-screen TV mounted above the fireplace, Petra shut it off. She motioned for Hypatia to join her on the couch. Upholstered in pale lilac, it made a pretty contrast in the mint-green and creamy-white room.

"I have something difficult to do tomorrow," Petra explained haltingly as Hypatia sank down on the edge of the sofa cushion. "I have to remove...someone from the project."

"Ah. That can't be pleasant."

Petra shook her head. "No. In fact, it's more awful than I thought it would be. Because he doesn't deserve it."

"Oh, dear."

"It's just one of those unhappy things," Petra said, shaking her head again, "but it's probably for the best."

"I can tell you're distressed by it, though."

"Yes, well, it comes with the job," Petra informed her.

"And this job is very important to you, isn't it, dear?" Hypatia asked, trying to understand.

"More important than you know!" Petra exclaimed. "Oh, Aunt Hypatia, this is my chance, my one real chance, to make something of myself!"

Shocked, Hypatia drew her spine straight. "Why, Petra Gayle Chatam," she scolded, "you are precious just as you are! How can you doubt it?"

"But I'm not like the rest of them!" Petra cried plaintively. "You know how dedicated my parents are."

"Yes, of course."

"And Asher is a wonderful lawyer."

"Without question."

Petra shot to her feet and began to pace. "And Phillip! He leads the life of an adventurer, climbing mountains and traveling all over the world."

"I pray for his safety all the time," Hypatia admitted with a nod.

"Even Dallas has always known where her place is in this world," Petra went on agitatedly. "She wasn't nine years old when she announced that she was going to be a schoolteacher."

"And so she is," Hypatia observed, still confused.

"But I," Petra declared, pausing to thump herself in the chest, "I've never had the slightest idea what I'm supposed to do."

"Is that all?" Hypatia blurted, oddly relieved.

"All?" Petra echoed. Shaking her head dejectedly, she dropped down beside Hypatia once more. "In my family, that's everything."

"Now, now," Hypatia soothed, taking her hand. "I know that's how it must seem, dear, but you're leaving out one very important ingredient."

"What's that?"

"God's guidance."

"But I've begged for God's guidance," Petra told her.

"Then you have to trust that He's leading you where He would have you go."

"I do," Petra assured her, squeezing her hand. "That's why this job is so important to me. I believe, I *know,* that He's led me to this point."

"Well, as long as you're following Him, you have nothing to fear," Hypatia said. "He'll give you everything you need."

Petra nodded. "You're right. I know it. I don't doubt Him. I doubt myself."

"You just stop that," Hypatia ordered, as if Petra was six again and would obey unhesitatingly.

Petra laughed. "I'll try."

"If it helps, dear," Hypatia told her, "I have every confidence in you."

Smiling, Petra hugged her, whispering, "Thank you."

Hypatia cleared her throat of the lump that had risen there, patted her niece, and rose smoothly to her feet. "I'll bid you good-night now." Bending, she kissed Petra on the forehead as she used to do when she and her sisters had tucked in the visiting children at night. "Sleep well."

"You, too."

Hypatia went to the door, but there she paused. "I'll pray for you tomorrow. And for whoever you must remove, poor man."

Petra bowed her head. "Thank you."

Nodding, Hypatia went out, determined to share her concerns with her sisters. They would pray, as always, and God would direct Petra's steps. As for that unfortunate man who did not deserve to lose his job, she would ask God to bless him in ways that he couldn't even imagine. Whoever he was, she hoped that he would feel the hand of God in his life and trust Him to provide his heart's desire.

Chapter Three

"It's not about his skills, Mr. Bowen," Petra said for perhaps the third time. "It's just a difference in management styles."

That excuse for removing Dale from the construction manager's position didn't sound any better now than the first time she'd used it, but she had little else to offer the man sitting across the battered desk from her. Walton Bowen was the rarest of persons, a truly nice individual. Nevertheless, he showed some irritation now, bracing his heavy hands on the arms of a chair that had seen better days.

"I've never met anyone who couldn't get along with my son," he insisted.

"It's not a matter of getting along, sir," she assured him. "As I said, it's just a—"

"Difference in management styles," said a wry, familiar voice from the doorway of the cluttered, dusty office.

She hadn't expected Dale to attend this meeting, but she wasn't surprised that he had. He was the construction manager on the project, after all. For the moment. She braced herself, tugging on the hem of her navy blue skirt, which she wore with a matching jacket and sensible flats. Dale's boots clumped across the wood floor, as the hydraulic arm on the heavy office door wheezed closed.

"If Anderton thinks he can work around the BCHS by getting me out of the way, he's wrong," Dale said to Petra, parking one hip on the corner of his father's desk and crossing his long legs at the ankles.

She couldn't deny either Dale's implication or his conclusion, but neither could she refuse a direct order. "He, *we,* feel that the work will go more smoothly with someone else as construction manager."

Dale folded his arms, looking down on her from his perch. "And I'm telling you that no one in this company knows the BCHS better or works closer with them than I do. No one in this *town,* for that matter."

"I'm sure you're right," she admitted. "Nevertheless…"

She didn't have to say more. Anger flashed across Dale's handsome face. Behind him, his father's chair creaked.

"I have a policy when it comes to disagreements, Ms. Chatam," he informed her. "Whenever we come to loggerheads in this office, we seek guidance in prayer."

Shocked, Petra tugged at her skirt again. She believed in prayer, of course, and frequently resorted to it. In private. But this was *business.* Still, she'd prayed about this very matter before she'd entered the large, metal building that housed Bowen & Bowen's offices and equipment.

Walt Bowen clasped his hands together atop the blotter on his desk and bowed his head, apparently waiting. After a moment, Dale shifted onto his feet. Turning, he joined Petra on the lumpy sofa. She bowed her head almost in self-defense, painfully aware of Dale as he leaned forward, braced his elbows upon his knees and knit his fingers together.

"Heavenly Father," Walt began, "it's not Your intention for Your children to be at odds, and as we sincerely seek Your will in all things, we come to You now for enlightenment and direction."

As he continued to speak, Petra felt her tension drain away

and a hopeful optimism begin to grow. Surely, this would all work out somehow. She tried to think what she might do to soften Garth's dislike of the man next to her, but God appeared to be way ahead of her.

No sooner were the "Amens" spoken than Dale Bowen sighed, swept his finger down his nose and said, "All right. You want me out of the way, I'll step aside. What we have to discuss now is who replaces me."

Petra slumped with relief and reached out to lay a hand on his strong arm before she could think better of the gesture. The man radiated heat like a log fire. She snatched her hand back. "Thank you."

He shrugged. "I still think it's a mistake."

"You may be right," she conceded. That changed nothing, however, and he obviously knew it.

"As far as your replacement," Walt said, spreading his big hands across the ink blotter, "that'll have to be me."

"No way," Dale objected, sitting back to cross one leg over the other. "You have enough on your plate. Jackie Hernandez can handle things."

"You sound like your mother," Walt grumbled.

"In other words, she'd agree with me," Dale retorted before glancing at Petra. "I'll explain things to Jackie myself."

"Isn't Mr. Hernandez the supervisor on-site?" Petra asked, wondering about that exchange between father and son.

"He is," Dale confirmed. "He's young, but don't be fooled by that. Jack knows what he's doing."

"My only concern is that he can handle the job," Petra replied earnestly.

"No worries there," Dale stated.

"Jack's a good man," Walt concurred.

"Then we're agreed," Petra said, getting to her feet. "Thank you, gentlemen."

Both men rose. Walton Bowen reached across his desk

to shake her hand, while Dale moved to hold open the door. Petra shot him a look of gratitude as she swiftly exited the room. She wasn't surprised when he followed her, but she couldn't help being a bit uncomfortable, even as he fell in beside her, strolling along as she walked through the cavernous building. Finally, she felt compelled to speak.

"I—I meant what I said before. It isn't personal." He snorted, so she added, "Not on my part." A slow smile spread across his face. Fascinated by the way the tip of his chin flattened and the green of his eyes intensified, she couldn't make herself look away.

"Good to know," he said softly.

She stumbled, suddenly feeling as if the ground shifted under her feet. His hand shot out, fastening around her upper arm.

"Careful," he said, drawing her to a halt.

The heat from his hand radiated up her arm and throughout her chest, stealing her breath. He released her the next instant, and she searched for something intelligent and safe to say. The only thing she could come up with was, "I like your dad."

He grinned. "Yeah. The worst anyone can say about my father is that he works too much."

She relaxed somewhat, saying lightly, "Wish I could adopt his prayer policy the next time Garth goes on a tear."

She smiled to herself, imagining the look on Garth's face if she suggested that they stop and pray together in the midst of one of his rants. But then the smile died as she realized that she had never before wondered about the state of Garth Anderton's soul. She would be very surprised if Walt Bowen was not intimately acquainted with the spiritual condition of each and every one of his employees. He probably prayed for them all daily and gently witnessed to every non-Christian among them. That's what her aunts would do. But all she'd thought about was what good Garth could do her career. Petra felt very small in that moment, very small, indeed.

"Does he do that often?" Dale asked.

She blinked up at him. "I'm sorry. I was thinking of something else. What do you want to know?"

"Does Anderton routinely go on a tear?" Dale clarified, frowning.

"Oh." She shrugged. "Not really. It's just that he's very… strong-willed."

"Used to getting his way, you mean."

"Well, he is the boss," she pointed out.

"I noticed. Have you been with him long?"

She shook her head. "Not him personally. I've been with the company about six months, but this is my first project working with Garth as his—"

"Special Assistant," Dale supplied.

Surprised at the bite in his tone, Petra frowned. "One of several," she clarified.

"Oh?" He sounded interested, so she went on.

"It's a temporary position, if you must know, a chance to prove yourself and move on to bigger things."

Dale folded his arms and cocked his head. "Such as?"

"Management. And then," she added enthusiastically, "acquisitions, I hope. He's taking the company international, eventually, and someone has to find properties in those exotic locales."

"And you want to be part of that?"

Surprised that he had to ask, she gave her head a wobbly shake. "Wouldn't you?"

"No. Especially not if it means living overseas."

Shocked, she backed up a step. "Why not?"

He dropped his hands to his waist and glanced around the building. "To put it simply, I'm a family man."

"But you're not even married!" she blurted.

He brought his gaze back to hers. "Not yet. But that

doesn't mean I don't have family. I'm in business with my father here. I have an apartment in my folks' house. I eat dinner nearly every night with them, my sister and her family. I wouldn't trade that for anything in the world—except…" Glancing down at his toes, he rocked back on his heels, then suddenly he looked her squarely in the eye again and said, "Except for a wife, home and family of my own." He smiled. "But that would just be adding to the family, wouldn't it?"

He seemed so sure of his place in the world, so confident that his life was on the right track; it left Petra feeling bereft and uncertain when she could least afford to be. Managing a smile, she reminded herself that she was finally getting it together, finally on her way to…what exactly? Financial success? A brilliant career? Happiness?

Gulping away her sudden doubts, she said what seemed most obvious. "The Bowens sound like a close family."

Dale nodded, clearly pleased. "We are. I always thought the Chatams were big on family, too. I mean, your aunts are so devoted to one another."

Petra smiled with genuine brightness. "Yes. They are." She felt her smile dim as she added, "Ours is just such a large family, though, that we all sort of go our own way."

"Maybe that's what it is then," he told her lightly. "Both of my parents are only children. Other than my grandparents, it's just us."

"Are your grandparents here, too?" she asked conversationally, turning for the door once more.

He kept pace with her. "Grandma and Grandpa Bowen are. They live out at The Haven," he told her, naming a private retirement complex. "Grandpa doesn't get out much anymore, and Grandma won't go anywhere without him. I try to visit them once or twice a week. Mom and sis are there nearly every day. Mom's parents, Grandma and Grandpa

Enderly, divide their time between here and Minnesota. They're here in the winter, there in the summer."

"Can't take the heat," Petra surmised distractedly, thinking about what her aunt had said about him being a "dutiful son." Apparently, he was just as devoted a grandson. A family man, who wouldn't want any job that took him away from those he loved.

As she knew too well, he didn't have to travel the world for a job like that. Her parents had worked long, grueling hours; as children, she and her brothers and sister had often gone days without seeing one or the other of them. Oh, there had been many exciting vacations to some of those exotic places she'd mentioned earlier. Too often, however, they as children had been admonished, usually by one of their many nannies, not to bother their busy parents with the small, everyday things that meant so much to kids.

Petra remembered one occasion especially, her first dance recital at the age of six. She'd been so nervous that her stomach had reacted poorly to her dinner, but the nanny had refused to call her mom, a pediatrician, saying that she would be in the audience when Petra performed, just in case Petra became ill. But "Dr. Maryanne" had spent only moments there that night. She'd been called to an emergency, unaware that her own child was embarrassing herself on stage by vomiting all over her patent-leather tap shoes.

That and other events had led Maryanne Chatam to eventually adopt a personal mantra that she repeated often to her daughters. "We've come a long way, but no woman can have it all, at least not all of the time."

"Or the cold," Dale said, and for the second time Petra had to shake her head apologetically.

"I'm sorry. What were we talking about?"

"Grandma and Grandpa Enderly," Dale informed her in an amused voice. "They don't like extreme temperatures."

"Right. Sorry," Petra apologized again. "Guess I'm just a little distracted this morning."

"Dumping project managers has that effect on some people," he quipped.

She had to laugh. "Apparently so."

They had reached the outside door at some point. A large, garage-type door on rollers, it stood open. She put out her hand. "Thank you for being so understanding."

He wrapped his big, warm hand around hers. "I'll be around when you need me." Not *if* but *when*.

She said nothing to that, just nodded, flashed a smile and walked out into the blazing June sun, pulling her hand from his. As she drove toward the hotel in her little silver coupe, she mused that, all in all, this onerous chore had gone far easier than she'd expected. She could thank the Bowens for that.

When she arrived at the hotel a few minutes later, Jackie Hernandez was waiting for her, but they barely got to speak before she had to take delivery of an office-full of electronic equipment and rented furniture. She spent the remainder of the morning setting up her office. Thankfully, Garth had returned to the home office in Austin for the day, so Petra didn't have to put up with him gloating about getting rid of Dale.

Maybe she was being unfair, though. Garth was a competitive sort, yes, but his business decisions were all about business. Usually. Nevertheless, Petra was glad that she didn't have to deal with him in person that day.

Jackie Hernandez came in about midafternoon again to let her know that he wasn't thrilled about his promotion.

"You're making a mistake to cut out Dale," he told her. "He *is* Bowen and Bowen now, and nobody knows these old buildings or BCHS like he does."

"I'm sure we'll manage," Petra told Hernandez. "Just let

me know immediately of any problems. *Before* you take them to Mr. Anderton."

Hernandez glumly nodded his understanding. "Yes, ma'am."

The problems began not half an hour later when the wrong supplies were delivered. Jackie pulled out the plans and argued with the deliveryman for ten minutes before the guy called Dale, only to concede afterward that Jackie was right.

"It'll go smoother next time," Petra told the new construction manager, praying that it would be so before hurrying off to begin setting up appointments to interview restaurant personnel.

Garth wanted the chef brought in on the ground floor, knowing that any chef worth his or her salt would insist that the kitchen be remodeled to personal specifications. They'd employed an agency to help them find likely candidates, and part of Petra's job was to weed through them so Garth could make the final choice. It turned out to be no small task.

Owing to her delayed start on the day, she got home too late for dinner that evening—but just in time to join the aunties at midweek prayer service. Tired to the bone, Petra would have loved to beg off, but one look at Aunt Hypatia's expectant face had her putting on a smile and trooping out the door again. She was glad that she went. Prayer, as the pastor reminded the congregation, is for the benefit of God's children rather than God Himself.

"Your Heavenly Father already knows your needs and desires, after all," he told them, "but by lifting them up to God, we gain strength in communion with Him, wisdom in His answers and much-needed perspective."

Petra wondered how God could know her needs and desires when she felt so unsure of them herself, but listening to all the requests for healing and rescue certainly put her personal troubles into perspective. As she bowed her head, she couldn't help thinking of Walt Bowen insisting that they pray together about Dale's position that morning, or of Dale sitting beside her on that couch with his head bowed unashamedly as Walt had sought guidance.

"Very solid people," Aunt Hypatia had called them, and she had been right.

Petra liked them. She wasn't entirely sure that she understood them, but she did like Walt and Dale Bowen. She wondered what Dale's mother and sister were like, then lost the thought in concentrated prayer. Afterward, she felt uplifted—but starved!

Hilda, bless her, had left a plate for Petra. She enjoyed the food in her room then left the remains in the old-fashioned dumbwaiter down the hall before climbing into the tall, four-poster bed. As she slipped off to sleep, she wondered if Dale had worked at Chatam House today. Very likely, he had. That meant he'd been right around the corner from this room. That seemed strange to her—and oddly significant.

His words drifted through her mind one last time.

"I'll be around when you need me."

She slept like the proverbial rock.

Petra arrived at the hotel early the next morning to find Garth already there. He asked right away how it went with Bowen. She replied simply that Jack Hernandez was the new construction manager.

"Excellent. Excellent," Garth said, rubbing his hands together. "In that case, I have a little bonus in the works for you." He rocked back on the heels of his Italian leather shoes and smiled. "It'll be ready later this afternoon, so I'll bring it by Chatam House this evening."

Deciding that she couldn't put him off any longer, Petra gave in graciously. "If you can be there by six, I'll let my aunts know that we'll be having company for dinner."

His smile widened. "Six, it is."

Petra turned the conversation to the pending chef interviews. By a quarter to five, exhausted from trying to stay a step ahead of Garth, she gratefully headed home to prepare for the evening ahead. She barely set foot on the landing upstairs when Dale appeared.

"I have something for you."

"Oh?" What was this, she wondered, gift Petra night?

He waved her over to look at a picture on his phone. "A contact of mine found these fixtures in a Chicago retrofit. He even found extra shades in the original boxes. What do you think?"

Petra looked at the wall-mounted brass-and-glass light fixtures and lifted an eyebrow. "They're lovely, but what are they for?"

He shot her a surprised look. "The missing hotel wall lamps. I counted fourteen."

Petra blinked. "Where are fourteen lamps missing?"

He jammed the phone into his hip pocket. "Hang on. I've got a copy of the hotel plans in the truck. Won't take a minute for me to show you exactly where the lamps go." He paused. "Unless you'd rather talk to Jackie about it. I can fill him in, and he can—"

She shook her head. That was just silly. Why insist on secondhand information? "Go on." She hurried toward her room, adding, "I'll just change and meet you back here."

"Okay." Dale smiled and shot down the stairs.

Petra ran to change. If they needed wall lamps, they needed wall lamps, for pity's sake. Hernandez would be handling the installation. What did it matter who told her about them?

She couldn't deny, though, that she'd much rather discuss the matter with Dale than the new project manager. Jackie was nice enough, but he seemed to blame her for Dale's removal and she couldn't very well tell him that Garth had insisted. Besides, something about Dale Bowen made her trust him. So what if he made her heart race just a little faster than normal? This was business. Just business.

Dale stood at the top of the stairs, a roll of blueprints in hand, when Petra reemerged from her room. She'd managed an amazing transformation in a short time, trading her severely tailored business suit for jeweled sandals, leggings and a shiny knit tunic in a shade of dark orange that made her eyes glow. She'd pulled the clasp from her hair and let it hang sleekly down her back.

"You look great," Dale heard himself blurt.

She stiffened slightly then smiled. "Thank you."

He had to force his mind back to the job at hand. "I've, uh, got a makeshift table in here." He carried the plans toward the unfinished suite. Petra followed. Unrolling the blueprints on a sheet of plywood balanced atop two sawhorses, he anchored one end with a hammer from his tool belt. "Okay, from the bottom floor up…"

Looking over his shoulder, she watched as he pointed out, numbered and marked with a pencil the placement of every fixture.

"I'll need those plans," she said when he finished. "Can you text me that photo so I can run it by Dexter?"

He took his phone out again. "Sure. What's your number?"

She told him, and he sent the photo. Hypatia showed up while Petra was saving the photo in her own cell phone.

"Petra, dear, your sister and a guest are downstairs."

"Already?" Petra yelped, glancing at the time. "I'm on my way. Thanks, Dale. I'll get back to you on this."

"Don't wait too long," he warned, rolling up the plans and handing them to her. "I've got these things on forty-eight-hour hold. After that, they go on the open market."

"You'll hear from me tomorrow," she promised, heading out the door.

Hypatia smiled at him but did not immediately turn to

follow her niece. Instead, to his surprise, she glanced around the room. "You've worked this space around the fireplace very well. Do you mind if I take a little tour?"

"Of course not. It's your house."

She smiled at that and asked a question, which he gladly answered despite the feeling that this was leading up to something else entirely. He didn't have to wait long to find out what it was.

"Mr. Bowen, might I ask a favor of you?"

He smiled. "Anything at all, ma'am. It's Dale, by the way. If you call me Mr. Bowen, I'll be looking around for my father."

"Dale, then." She folded her hands and squared her silk-clad shoulders before saying, "Would you mind very much staying for dinner tonight?"

Taken aback, Dale felt his jaw drop. "Ma'am?"

"We have so missed Jessa and Hunter," she said, "not to mention dear Garrett, and our Petra tires of being the only young person in attendance, I'm sure. But most of all, frankly, we could use a man to balance the table. We would be most grateful."

"I—I see."

He knew that the Chatam triplets were "old-world," as Garrett put it, but Dale had never known anyone who worried about one gender or another being outnumbered at the dinner table. Still, he was tempted, if only because of Hilda's cooking. But of course, it wasn't only that. He thought of how pretty Petra had looked just now and felt his smile intensify, but then he frowned again, gesturing at his clothes. They were clean, thanks to the coveralls that he usually wore, but they weren't exactly up to Chatam standards.

"I'd have to run home and change."

"Oh, no, you're fine," Hypatia assured him. "Garrett came to the table in jeans all the time."

Knowing his friend Garrett Willows, Dale could certainly

believe that. "Well, if you're sure, then I'd be very pleased to stay. Just let me spruce up a bit and make a couple of quick calls."

Hypatia literally beamed. "Wonderful. We'll await you downstairs."

"Yes, ma'am, and thank you."

"Oh, no, thank *you,* Dale."

She went out, leaving Dale to mentally scratch his head. Well, that beat all. He pulled his phone from his pocket once more. Petra tired of being the only young person at the table, did she? They had to "balance the table"? He shook his head as he called his mother to let her know he wouldn't be home for dinner that evening. Then he quickly dialed up his good buddy Garrett to see if he could offer any enlightenment about what might really be behind this unexpected dinner invitation.

Chapter Four

After stowing the plans in her room, Petra all but flew down the stairs, hitting the foyer in a near-run. She drew up only as she reached the door to the parlor and calmed herself, trying not to imagine what her sister might be saying to her boss. Why did Dallas have to choose tonight of all nights to drop by for dinner? Her baby sister was prone to outlandish behavior and odd ideas. Their brothers often remarked that she wasn't Odelia's namesake for nothing.

Petra quickly found that Garth, as usual, had taken the entire gathering in hand. He sat in a gold-and-yellow-striped armchair, leaning forward slightly as he winked at Odelia, who was already twittering like a tree full of robins.

"A very fetching bride," he was saying. "Blast my luck for coming along too late."

Even Magnolia chuckled at that, or it may have been the quivering of the green ostrich feather boa twined about Odelia's head that tickled the usually taciturn sister. Surprisingly, Odelia appeared to be wearing a ring of grass in her hair, which was surely meant to somehow complement the pebble print of her caftan. The significance of the huge twiggy things poking out from her earlobes confused Petra until she realized that they were made of wood. This, then, was

Odelia's homage to nature. Or ground cover. She couldn't be sure which, but then she was more interested in the red-head parked in the side chair next to Garth. Dallas looked as pleased as a cat in cream.

"It was too late fifty years ago," she said in reply to Garth's quip. She tossed her blazing-red head in the direction of the settee, where Kent sat with one beefy arm draped about Odelia's plump shoulders. "I think Kent beat you to the mark before you were even born."

"Missed it by more than a decade," Garth replied smoothly. Dallas arched a slender, carroty brow speculatively and parked her hands at the impossibly narrow waist of the simple, lime-green sundress that she wore. Her amber gaze lit on Petra then, and she smiled wide enough to break a tooth.

"Hey, sis! Guess who's staying for dinner?"

"That would be me," Garth quipped, turning his head to greet Petra. He rose as she moved forward.

"And me!" Dallas crowed.

"You look very nice," he said to Petra. "Take my seat."

"No, no, I'll share with my sister," Petra told him, sliding past him to perch on the narrow wood arm of Dallas's chair. She was down before poor Kent managed to make it fully upright. His behind hadn't touched the sofa cushion again before Dallas addressed Garth.

"Is it true that you have private apartments in every one of your hotels?"

"And at my corporate headquarters," he confirmed.

"But you don't have a house?" she pressed.

His smiled tightened. "Not any longer."

What he meant was not since the last divorce. Petra smoothly changed the subject.

"I believe you said you had something for me."

His smile relaxed again, and he reached into the pocket of his suit jacket. "Ah, yes. Had it inscribed just today." He pulled a long, flat box from his coat and opened it. Inside lay a very expensive watch with a capital *A* superimposed over a capital *V* on the gold face. He turned it over so she could see the inscription.

"'To Petra,'" Dallas read aloud, "'for a job well done. Garth.'"

"It's very nice," Petra said as Garth took her wrist and fastened the watch around it.

"What does the *A* and *V* mean?" Odelia asked, leaning forward to get a better look.

"Anderton Vail," Garth answered. "It's the logo for the hotel."

Petra shook her hand so the thick chain slid around and the face, which was circled in tiny diamonds, became visible.

"Thank you," she said, feeling more than the simple weight of the gold. The watch seemed to be an entirely appropriate business gift, but she'd have preferred a mundane raise in pay or even a sincere "Atta' girl." Or, better yet, nothing at all. It felt wrong to accept a gift for firing a man, though she hadn't really done any such thing and this, she feared, had less to do with business than it should.

When Hypatia appeared a few minutes later, Petra felt obligated to show off the watch again and even more conflicted about it. She welcomed the interruption when Chester, the houseman, came to announce that dinner could be served at any time.

"We'll need a few more minutes, Chester," Hypatia replied calmly.

She went on admiring Petra's watch and asking questions about the logos of the other Anderton hotels. Garth was in the midst of listing the hotels and explaining their individual logos when Dale Bowen walked into the room. His unruly hair appeared freshly combed, and he'd somehow managed to shave. Petra supposed that, like many men, he carried a battery-operated razor. She also supposed that he'd been invited to dinner!

Her assumption proved entirely correct when Hypatia smiled and said, "We can go in now, as we're all acquainted."

"I'm not acquainted!" Dallas exclaimed, leaping to her feet with a frown.

"That's right. You weren't at Garrett's wedding dinner," Hypatia said, going on to make the introduction without apology. "Mr. Dale Anthony Bowen, please meet my niece, Miss Dallas Odelia Chatam. Dallas is Petra's younger sister. Now we may go in."

With that, she turned and took Dale's arm, lest anyone be in doubt that he was her personal guest and should be treated accordingly. Garth cast Dale a stormy glance as the latter escorted Hypatia from the room. Petra realized suddenly that she should have told Garth that Dale worked on the premises, but it hadn't even occurred to her to do so. She'd assumed that the less said about Dale Bowen the better. Wrong.

Recovering quickly, Garth hurried to offer one arm to Petra and the other to Magnolia, leaving Kent with both Odelia and Dallas, who tossed her short, bright curls as she took the older man's arm. Petra sensed her little sister's dismay, but she couldn't imagine why Dallas should be discomfited. Garth's reaction she could understand. He'd had no idea that Bowen worked here, let alone that he was on the premises, but Dallas presented a puzzle. Who could tell, though, what went on in her little sister's head?

Besides, the bigger question was, why had Hypatia invited Dale to dinner? Garth asked the same question obliquely as they followed Hypatia and Dale down the west hall toward the dining room.

"I must say I'm surprised to find Bowen on the guest list."

"Oh, Dale works here," Magnolia supplied. "He's creating a new suite upstairs for Odelia and Kent."

"I see."

Garth turned a cold glare on Petra, who sighed inwardly. Obviously, she'd made a big mistake. She wondered if he'd take back his watch and almost hoped that he would. Except that she needed this job, she reminded herself. She had plans, big plans, and the promised promotion was crucial to them.

"It's the first time he's ever been to dinner, though," Magnolia went on blithely. "Well, except for Garrett's wedding dinner. You haven't met dear Garrett, have you, Mr. Anderton?"

"I have not, ma'am."

"We'll have to arrange that."

"Garrett Willows will be supplying flowers and plants for the hotel," Petra put in. "I'm sure you'll meet at some point."

Magnolia exclaimed happily about that, describing Willow Tree Place to Garth as everyone got seated around the dining table. As soon as they had all found chairs, Hypatia smiled from her customary spot at the head of the table and looked to Dale, who had taken a place across from Dallas between Magnolia and Odelia. Petra, meanwhile, sat flanked by her sister on one side and Garth on the other.

"Dale," Hypatia asked smoothly, "would you honor us by saying the blessing?"

"Happy to," he replied, bowing his head.

If he was surprised, he certainly didn't show it, but Petra saw Kent glance at Odelia, who shrugged slightly before dropping her chin. When Petra herself glanced at Garth, she saw he'd been caught off guard and was watching everyone else for a clue as to what to do. She quickly folded her hands in her lap and bowed her head as Dale began to speak.

"Father God, we come in humble gratitude for the food we are about to receive from Your great bounty, and we ask Your blessing on those who have prepared and provided it for our enjoyment. May Your Spirit nourish our souls as this meal nourishes our bodies. These things we pray in the name of Your Holy Son, Jesus the Christ. Amen."

As a chorus of "Amens" echoed around the table, Chester and the housemaid, Carol, came in bearing trays of food, which they placed, dish by dish, on the table. Plates of cheese and crisp cucumbers served with spicy mustard came first, followed by platters of pan-grilled chicken breasts and baked sweet potatoes. A bowl of corn and an asparagus casserole came next, with hot sesame bread last.

Garth took one bite of his chicken and went into raptures. "What is this? It's delicious!"

"I think Hilda, our cook, finishes it off with apple cider vinegar," Magnolia told him.

"We should steal her for the hotel restaurant," he said to Petra. Everyone laughed, but Petra knew that he was half-serious. She knew, as well, that he'd have better luck stealing the gold out of Fort Knox.

Garth promptly set out to charm everyone at the table, talking about the various chefs at his hotels and their peculiar personalities. Completely monopolizing the conversation, he had everyone chuckling at his witticisms and stories. Petra noticed that Dale did manage to get in a few pithy rejoinders, however.

Once, Garth told a long, involved story about a certain head chef who had blown off successful careers in finance, engineering and real estate only to wind up a top cook. "So I ask him," Garth finished, "why cooking? He sighs and says, 'I was looking for something I could fail at.'"

"Should've tried construction," Dale quipped dryly as the laughter waned. "It's easy to fail at that."

"Not that you have ever done so, I'm sure," Hypatia decreed from the head of the table. "Nor are you likely to."

"From your lips to God's ears, ma'am," he returned softly.

Garth cleared his throat and launched into another tale, one that had them all hanging on his every word, about a woman who swore she'd learned to cook so she could poison her abusive husband, but then she fell in love with cooking.

Her husband was so impressed that he stopped beating her and gained three hundred pounds.

"Died of a heart attack at forty-four," Garth said. "His family still believes she got away with murder."

Dallas leapt into the conversational fray by addressing Dale directly. "I think he did it to himself, don't you? Unless she was shoving food down his throat."

"Makes you think, though," Dale said with a straight face. "I figured Hilda was always trying to feed me because she likes me, but maybe I'm on her hit list."

The aunties and Kent all laughed and chorused, "Me, too!"

Garth showed his teeth in what was surely meant to be a smile, and began regaling his captive audience with descriptions of dishes he'd enjoyed in faraway places. Finally, Chester served dessert. After wolfing his down, Dale rose, thanked his hostesses and took his leave, but not before he sent Petra a crooked smile. She wanted to follow him and apologize for… Well, she didn't know what she wanted to apologize for; she did know that the evening had been excruciating. Of course, she stayed in her seat and continued to smile lamely when a response seemed necessary, privately writhing all the while.

After what seemed like hours, Garth finally took his leave, too. First, though, he kissed the hands of all the aunties, clapped Kent on the shoulder with manly bonhomie and bowed to Dallas before appropriating Petra and leading her to the front door.

"Lovely evening," he said conversationally. "Delicious meal. Delightful company." He leaned forward then and whispered in her ear, "How did I do?"

She just barely tamed an eye-roll that would have done Magnolia proud. "You don't need me to tell you that you charmed them."

He beamed then muttered, "Bowen was a surprise."

"Wasn't he?"

Those pale gray eyes narrowed. "How do you like the watch?"

"It's beautiful. Thank you."

Smiling, he chucked her under the chin. "My pleasure. I'd do a lot more for you, you know, if you'd let me."

Without a word, she stepped aside, opened the door and held it for him. He paused a moment, as if waiting for her to precede him through it, but she just smiled, not about to go out on that shadowy porch with him. His mouth set grimly, but then he put on his smile again.

"See you tomorrow."

"Tomorrow," she echoed cheerily, and a few blessed seconds later closed the door on his back.

The instant she turned toward the stairs, Dallas pounced, obviously having followed them as far as the cloakroom beneath the staircase.

"Is he not delicious?"

For one insane moment, Petra thought she was referring to Dale. "I didn't know you had a thing for—"

"Not me!" Dallas laughed. "I mean for you. Garth Anderton is the perfect man for you, sister."

Garth? Petra's jaw dropped. "Are you out of your mind? He's my boss."

"So? All to the good, I say," Dallas gushed excitedly, "and you have to admit that I have a sense about these things. I was the one, after all, who knew that Aunt Odelia and Kent still had a thing for each other."

Ignoring that last statement, which was sadly true, Petra shook her head. "I am not interested romantically in Garth Anderton."

"Oh, please," Dallas scoffed. "He's gorgeous, engaging, thoughtful, clever…" All true of course, Petra admitted secretly. "And rich! Just look at that watch."

"The *company* paid for this," Petra pointed out, holding aloft her wrist.

"He *is* the company."

"Listen to me, Dallas," Petra commanded firmly, grasping her sister by the shoulders. "I am *not* romantically interested in Garth Anderton."

Dallas sniffed, lifting her cleft chin. "Whyever not?" She suddenly shrugged out of Petra's grasp, her eyes widening. "It's that carpenter! How can you be more interested in him than Garth Anderton?"

"I'm not interested in either one of them!" Dallas insisted. "I'm focused on my career."

Dallas snorted delicately. "As if."

"I am!"

"Oh, come on, sis. Aren't you the least bit attracted to him?"

"Which one? I mean, no! I work for Garth Anderton. End of story. And I barely even know Dale Bowen."

"Well, keep it that way with Bowen," Dallas advised, "and Anderton will take care of himself. He was practically drooling over you at the table. You could be the next Mrs. Anderton before the first guest checks into the hotel."

"I don't want to be the *next* Mrs. Anderton!"

"Why not? It isn't as if you've had a burning need your whole life to manage a hotel."

"Oh, you're hopeless!" Petra cried, all the more incensed because Dallas was half-right. She'd never thought a thing about hotel management until she'd gone to work for the Anderton chain, but this was the best chance that she'd come across yet to have a real career. She'd prayed for this, begged for it, and she wasn't going to blow it now. "I'm not going to listen to any more of your nonsense. Good night to you."

Whirling, she stomped over to the stairs and climbed them at a trot. Once upstairs, she closed herself inside her room and plopped down onto the fringed, pale lilac brocade couch,

putting her hands to her head. The watch slid a couple inches
down her arm. This, she told herself fiercely, was proof that
she was on the right track. Oh, she knew that Garth was in
pursuit of her, if only out of habit, but she could handle him.
Dale Bowen, on the other hand…

She admitted bleakly just how very attractive she did find
him. In fact, she found it impossible to think that her sister
didn't secretly judge him the better catch. Okay, so he wasn't
rich, but he seemed to do okay, and he obviously loved his
work. A self-described family man, he would be a good husband and father, the sort who was always there when needed,
the kind she'd dreamed of as a little girl.

At the dinner table tonight, Petra hadn't been able to keep
her gaze from wandering over him. Worse, every time he'd
smiled or nodded at Dallas, Petra had felt a pang of jealousy,
as if her sister might steal him away, a ridiculous idea since
he wasn't Petra's to begin with, and never would be.

She knew her limitations. Having watched her mother try
to juggle family and career, Petra realized that she couldn't
do both, and career was what she'd always wanted, so marriage was out of the question.

"Focus," she told herself. "Focus on the job."

Just the job. Always the job.

Feeling calmer, she nodded—but why, she wondered,
now that she stood poised on the brink of achieving all she
wanted, did it suddenly seem…less than anticipated?

Halfway home, Dale realized that he'd left his tools in the
suite at Chatam House. He made a point of carrying everything away with him at the end of every workday, purely as
a gesture of respect for the Chatam sisters and the sanctity
of their home. Obviously, Hypatia's unexpected invitation
had thrown him off his stride. Dinner, on the other hand,
had completely destroyed his equilibrium.

Oh, not the meal itself. Hilda was every bit the cook that

everyone claimed. Her food proved delicious. No, what had ruined it for him was the company. Garth Anderton, to be specific. All night long, Dale had felt an alarming need to punch the blowhard. Not a particularly Christian attitude. Maybe if he hadn't gone into that room expecting basically to have Petra to himself—discounting the Chatam sisters and Kent, of course—he'd have tolerated Anderton's presence better. Or maybe not. He figured he'd have been disappointed either way.

What, he wondered, had put the notion into Garrett's head that Hypatia was playing matchmaker? Clearly, her only concern had been providing Garth Anderton, not Petra, with the company of a man nearer his age than good old Kent, who could rarely take his attention off Odelia. No, however well he knew the Chatam sisters, Garrett had gotten this one wrong, and Dale couldn't believe how let down he felt about that.

He wouldn't go back to Chatam House now, he decided, not at this hour of the evening. Instead, he'd make his apologies tomorrow, and should Hypatia ever invite him to dinner again, he wouldn't let his imagination run away with him. He would, in fact, politely decline. From the moment he'd realized that Anderton was on the guest list, Dale had felt terribly out of place, sitting there in his work clothes while everyone else wore their expensive duds. Even Odelia, as wild as that getup had been, had worn her money, as it was said, for all to see.

Dale had never in his life yearned for fancy suits or expensive accessories. That just wasn't him. Might as well face the fact that the Chatams were silk, especially Petra, while he was homespun. As sleek and shiny as a new sports car, she'd looked exactly right sitting next to that wealthy, if bombastic, man. She certainly wasn't made for the likes of a glorified carpenter, and he must've been hallucinating to entertain the notion that Hypatia Chatam, of all people, would ever think so.

Henceforth, he'd remember what it felt like to sit there in his jeans while Garth oozed charm out of his expensive suit. Dale had even noticed Petra and her sister looking at him from time to time as if to ask what he was doing there. Once or twice, he'd thought Petra had looked at him differently, almost as if she'd felt sorry for him or maybe even shared his discomfort. Well, he didn't need her pity, and he was undoubtedly wrong about the latter.

He didn't fit in with the likes of the Chatams and Anderton. He'd do well to remember that, and while he was at it, he'd do well to remember that Garth Anderton had given Bowen & Bowen a rare and stellar opportunity, one that could make all the difference where his father's health was concerned. Dale didn't have to like Garth to respect what he'd achieved in his life or realize that he'd been used of God to answer very specific prayers. So, he'd do what he could from the sidelines to help Jackie and put pretty Petra Chatam from his mind. He prayed the latter wouldn't be as difficult as he feared, but knowing that she was out of his league didn't make him like her any less. He comforted himself with the knowledge that God surely had a woman in mind for him, someone who valued the durability of denim more than the shine of satin.

Thursday became a giant headache for Petra, with one problem after another cropping up at the hotel and Garth growling like an old bear awakened too early from hibernation. Friday proved worse. Garth had to make a mad dash to Cripple Creek, Colorado, to take care of a catastrophe at the hotel there when a water tank on the roof of the building had flooded the floors below. No sooner had he gone than a trio of inspectors from the Historical Society showed up. The man carried a magnifying glass, for pity's sake, the better to find reasons for complaint, which the two elderly women dutifully noted on their clipboards.

To top off the week, someone discovered that the electricians were using wire that had been recalled by the manufacturer, meaning that everything they'd done to date would have to be torn out and installed again. So much for staying on schedule.

Petra's mood could only be described as black when she encountered Dale on the stairway at Chatam House that evening. When she realized that he intended to pass her by with nothing more than a nod, her composure cracked.

She heard herself snap, "You could at least say hello."

He paused with one foot poised to step down and turned his head to look at her. "Hello."

She immediately felt contrite and looked away. "Sorry. I'm in a lousy mood."

"I wasn't trying to be rude," he said softly.

"Of course you weren't. Like I said, lousy mood." She waved him on his way with a sweep of her hand, but then she couldn't resist exclaiming, "It's as if everything that could go wrong today did!" She shook her head, muttering, "But that's not your problem. I made sure of that."

"You were only carrying out Anderton's orders," he said gently.

"Yes. I was," she affirmed, feeling a bit mollified. "Still, it's not your problem. I'm sure you don't want to hear about it."

He said nothing to that, just took the next step. But then he paused, as if he couldn't quite make himself go on down those stairs, and put his back to the railing. "Actually, Jackie already told me about the wiring."

She threw up her hands. "There goes the schedule! And my promotion."

"Not necessarily," he told her soothingly. "I'm going to talk to the electrical subcontractor and get him to go to the supplier with me. This was their error. I think we can convince them to pay overtime so the electricians can get caught up. Meanwhile, Jackie's bringing in a generator and all the extra cords he can find. Work will go on."

Relieved, she breathed, "Thank you."

Dale shrugged, smiling, and it occurred to her that he was, indeed, there when she needed him. She gulped, grateful beyond words. The least she could do was apologize for dinner the other night.

"I'm sorry about what happened at dinner."

"What do you mean?" he asked, lifting his eyebrows.

"Garth expects to dominate every conversation," she said, "but he usually lets other people get a word in edgewise here or there."

Dale regarded her frankly. "Anderton was trying to impress you."

"No!" she denied instantly. Then she grimaced. "Well, everyone. He likes to charm everyone, but not me in particular."

Dale tilted his head skeptically. "If you say so."

"No, really," she insisted. "And anyway, I'm not...impressed." Why she'd felt the need to say that, she wasn't sure, but there it was.

Dale's glowing green gaze held hers for several long seconds, a lopsided smile slowly stretching his lips. Then he nodded and lightly said, "Well, I am. Anderton is an impressive man. He's accomplished a lot, experienced a lot."

"My sister says the same thing, more or less," Petra muttered.

Dale shrugged. "Not surprised he's her type."

"*Her* type," Petra had to say, "not mine."

Dale Bowen tilted his head again, asking softly, "No? What is your type, then, Petra?"

She realized suddenly that she'd somehow gotten herself

into dangerous territory. "Oh. I don't have one. I'm focused on my career."

"I can see that," he said, as if he'd thought about it.

Petra found herself suddenly breathless, but she attempted to ignore that fact. "That's why I am...so very grateful for your assistance...with the electrical stuff."

He smiled warmly. "No problem."

"You're as good as your word," she told him. "Thank you."

He stood there a moment longer then suddenly looked away. "Well, I guess I'll be seeing you around."

"Yes," she said, oddly relieved by that.

"So long then."

"Bye," she returned, and he started down the stairs once more. He glanced back as he rounded the curve in the staircase, and she lifted a hand in farewell.

"I'll be around when you need me," he'd said, and he'd proved it twice over already. She wished it didn't make her feel so glad, and she couldn't help wondering when she would next need his help. She very much feared that needing Dale Bowen could quickly become a habit.

Chapter Five

Business drove Petra to Dale for help the following Wednesday.

She'd caught a glimpse of him in church on Sunday. He'd been with his father and, ostensibly, his mother, a short, plump woman with apple cheeks and silver-shot blond hair, which she wore wound into a bun on top of her head. Walt Bowen had waved, while Dale had offered a smiling nod of acknowledgment. He had not approached her in any other way and had hardly seemed aware of her presence after that one small greeting.

That smarted a bit, and Petra couldn't figure out why. It wasn't as if they were *friends,* after all. They were business associates, for pity's sake. Just business associates. Nevertheless, she knew that she would go to him for advice as soon as the BCHS representative dropped off the punch list of changes that had to be made "before work could proceed."

Without a word to anyone else, Petra packed her briefcase with all the necessary papers, grabbed a roll of blueprints and set out for Chatam House. It didn't occur to her until she was climbing the stairs toward the second floor of the mansion that Dale might not be there. Oh, well, she decided, if she didn't find him here, she'd track him down by phone.

She need not have worried. As soon as she walked into the suite, he looked up from the heavy antique door hinge that he was rubbing to a bronze glow and immediately laid it aside. Wiping his hands on a faded red shop cloth, he glanced at the briefcase and roll of plans.

"What's going on?" he asked.

"You were right," she told him baldly. "The BCHS has more than a few issues with our renovations and is threatening to bring work to a halt."

"Let's take a look," was his calm reply.

He nodded at the makeshift table over which he worked, and Petra began spreading out her papers. As she did so, she mused that he was, true to his word, once again right where she needed him to be, and she couldn't help hoping that would always be the case.

"This one is easy enough," Dale said, pecking an item on the punch list with the tip of his forefinger. "I'll show Jackie what to do." He went on, offering possible solutions to every complaint on the list. When he was done, he'd whittled the thing down to half a dozen sticking points. "I'll call Tansy Burdett, the head of the BCHS, and see if we can set up a meeting to work out the rest of this. Meanwhile I'll go over everything else, in detail, with Jackie."

Petra sighed with relief. "Thank you," she said fervently. Her stomach growled audibly at that moment. Embarrassed, she pressed a hand to her flat middle. "Oh, my!"

Dale pulled out his phone and checked the time, surprised to see that the lunch hour had long since passed. He was hungry himself, but then he generally always was.

"Goodness. I didn't mean to be so long-winded."

"No apology necessary," she insisted, lifting a palm. "You missed your lunch helping me solve yet another dilemma."

Shaking his head, Dale pulled over a battered folding chair and placed it next to the table. "I haven't missed anything." He brought his lunchbox to the table. "Seems only fair that I share," he told her, pulling out two sandwiches, a bag of chips, another of chopped carrots, cucumbers and celery, a banana and a brownie as big as a floor tile. His mom did know what he liked.

"I can't take your lunch," Petra protested, even as she moved over to the chair.

He hopped up onto the makeshift table, dropped a wrapped sandwich into her lap and popped open the chip bag. "More like a late afternoon snack now," he said, chuckling. "If I eat the whole lot of goodies this late, I won't want any dinner."

It was a blatant lie. With his metabolism, he could eat twenty-four hours a day. She didn't seem inclined to argue further, however. He unwrapped his sandwich and picked up half of a thick stack of bread, cheese, lettuce and meat.

"Hope you like roast beef," he said before biting off a huge chunk.

"Mmm," came her answer, her mouth being too full to speak.

He smiled and chewed. They ate in companionable silence for several minutes before Petra swallowed and waved a hand at the food scattered across the table. "Do you always eat this much?"

Nodding, he reached for the banana, peeled it, and broke it in two pieces, offering one to her. She shook her head. "I've always been a big eater," he told her. "If I miss a couple of meals, I have to take in my belt a few notches."

"That's just not fair," she drawled with a comical scowl, making him laugh.

"You've got nothing to worry about," he said off-handedly. "You're slim."

Great. Now they both knew that he'd checked her out.

She cleared her throat and murmured, "Thank you." Then she added, "I was starving."

"Doesn't compare to Hilda's fare," he commented lightly, concentrating on his banana, "but it'll keep you going until dinner."

"Which isn't too far away," she said, looking at her fancy watch. She glanced nervously around the room as if looking for a way out, only to sit up straight and take another long perusal. What she saw seemed to please her. "This is lovely. I haven't really had a chance to pay attention before now. The mauve is gorgeous with the cream-white woodwork."

"Well, I can't take credit for the colors," he told her, glad for the change of subject. "Odelia chose those."

"Really?" Petra said, blinking at him. "Auntie Od chose something this classy?"

Dale nearly fell off the table laughing. Petra blanched, but then she laughed, too.

"You really call her Auntie Od?" he asked.

"Not to her face," Petra admitted sheepishly, "and I shouldn't have said that. She's such a sweetheart."

"She is," Dale agreed. "Very sweet. Very kind. But then all of your aunts are." He hopped off the table. "Before you beat yourself up too badly, though, come have a look in here."

Petra got up and followed him into a surprisingly small bedroom, which had been painted pale purple. Dale glanced back and crooked a finger at her before stepping up to a door. He crooked a finger at her, waiting until she drew near to throw open that door.

"I'm guessing it's the largest bathroom in Chatam House," he said.

Without the fixtures, which had yet to be set, the room seemed cavernous, despite the yards of fuchsia tile and sunny yellow paint that overwhelmed the observer.

"Oh, my word," Petra gasped.

"I'm saving the best for last," he announced, grinning. Grabbing her by the hand, he hauled her through another open doorway and into the near total darkness of the closet before reaching for the light switch. A pair of crystal chandeliers lit up the garishly painted walls. Odelia had insisted that the closet be painted in wide bands of color that roughly corresponded to those of her wardrobe. Petra stood with her mouth open for a good minute before he enlightened her.

"It's color-coded so Carol will know where to hang Odelia's clothes."

"Of course!" Petra squeaked, slapping a hand over her mouth to muffle her laughter. "It's so…so…Odelia!" she managed, looking up at the chandeliers.

Dale grinned ear-to-ear. "Kent comes in here a couple times a day. He says this closet makes him happy, but I think it's indulging her that makes him happy. Did you know he's planning to build her a swimming pool as a wedding present?"

"No!" Petra gasped, spinning to face him.

Dale nodded. "He showed me the plans, but it's a big secret, so don't tell." To reinforce that, he thoughtlessly placed a finger over her lips. His gaze instantly locked there.

Electricity suddenly sizzled in the air as he imagined kissing her. Dale jerked his hand away from her, shifting his gaze aside. He shouldn't have touched her, hadn't imagined such a strong, visceral reaction. Beside him, he heard her gulp.

After a moment, she whispered, "I won't say a word, I promise."

He turned as casually as he could manage and led the way out of there, shaken clear to his bones.

"I think we should meet with the BCHS here at Chatam House," Petra said, relieved that her voice did not betray the quivering that she felt inside as she followed Dale back to the sitting room of the suite. She didn't really know what had happened there in the closet, but she knew it didn't have anything to do with *business,* and that she desperately needed to put whatever was going on between her and Dale Bowen back on a firm business footing.

"That sounds like a good idea," Dale replied after a moment, gazing straight ahead. "Chatam House is neutral ground, so to speak. But are you sure your aunts won't mind with all the wedding preparations going on and everything?"

"I'll okay it with them," Petra answered, "but I think it will be fine. It's not like they have to participate in the meeting."

"I'll call BCHS then and find out how quickly we can meet."

"Good."

"Meanwhile," Dale said, coming to a halt beside the saw-horse table where they'd eaten earlier, "I'll get with Jackie and explain how these other issues are to be handled. It's mostly a matter of technique." She watched him stack her papers and roll up the plans, his large, capable hands moving with a natural efficiency.

"Just how did you happen to learn all these historical techniques, anyway?" Petra asked, curious.

He shrugged. "My grandpa used to work on these old buildings around town, and I've always liked to know how to do things, so when he offered to teach me some of the old techniques, I was happy to learn. That spurred an interest in the old ways, which were, frankly, often superior to how we do things now, so when I got into college I made a study of it, but I'm still learning all the time. Now," he said, finally looking at her again, "it's my turn to ask a question."

The odd moment seemed to have passed, so she nodded her head. "All right."

"How did you get into hotel management?"

Petra mentally cringed. She hated for him to know how feckless she'd been to this point, but she didn't want to lie to him. "I stumbled into it," she finally admitted. "I was just looking for something to do with a business management degree and got hired on at Anderton. When I realized that Anderton's business model is to buy old hotels of some historical significance and restore or upgrade them, I naturally thought of the Vail. I worked up a prospectus and proposed it. Garth eventually agreed then promoted me when the sale was completed and promised to make me the hotel manager when the renovations are finished. *If* I can somehow make them happen on time and under budget."

Dale sucked in a deep breath. "I see. So both our futures are riding on this project."

"What do you mean?" she asked, shocked. "How is your future dependent on this job?"

"Oh, I'll be fine regardless," he said with a wave of one hand. "Dad is the issue. Twice in the last three years, he's worked himself into a state of exhaustion. I'm talking hospitalization. And it's affected his heart. That's why I decided against taking a second degree and came home to work in the family business. The doctor fears for his overall health if this continues, his heart in particular. Mom wants him to retire, and I agree that he should, but he's not even sixty yet, and we have a cash flow problem. With this economy, who doesn't? The hotel renovation could be the key to him being able to step back, for a while at least."

Petra shook her head sorrowfully. "Dale, I had no idea."

"Why would you?" he asked.

"You were considering an advanced degree program?" she asked, harking back to what he'd said earlier. "In what?"

"Archaeology." He gave her a wry, lopsided grin and waved a hand around. "You think these building techniques are old!"

Before she could reply to that, his phone rang. He slipped it out of his back pocket and lifted it to his ear.

"This is Dale." After listening a moment, he glanced at the front of the phone then put it back to his ear. "Mom, I'm sorry. I had no idea it had gotten so late."

Petra glanced at her watch. "Good grief!"

"For pity's sake, don't wait on me," Dale said into the phone. "Y'all go ahead and eat. I'll get something in town. Thanks, Mom." He ended the call and flapped his arms in consternation. "First lunch and now dinner!"

"I'm so sorry," Petra apologized, appalled. "I didn't mean to keep you so late!"

"Not your fault," he protested. "I'm the one who insisted on showing you the rest of the suite."

She shook her head. "No, no, I've taken nearly your whole day. The least I can do is see to it that you get a decent dinner. I'm sure my aunts would be pleased if you joined us, and I know there will be plenty of food."

He shook his head. "Oh, I couldn't."

"I promise Garth won't be here," she teased, "or my sister, so far as I know."

Chuckling, he rubbed his chin, where a charming five o'clock shadow had bloomed, Petra realized. How could he look so handsome while in need of a shave?

"Well..." he hedged, "if you're sure it wouldn't be an imposition..."

"Not at all," she vowed.

He grinned. "In that case, why not? I confess I'm curious to see what Hilda has prepared."

Delighted, Petra laughed. She couldn't help herself. "I'll run down and let the others know. Then I ought to have just enough time to change into more comfortable clothing."

"I have to put away all this stuff and get myself together, too," he told her, quickly moving to do that.

"Meet you on the landing in ten minutes," she called, hurrying away. He flashed her a smile.

Halfway down the stairs, she realized what she'd done. So much for putting them back on a strictly business footing! But really, not inviting him to dinner would have been rude. First, she'd removed the man as the project construction supervisor, then she'd run to him every time she had a problem, which he routinely found ways to solve, and in the process, she'd ruined both his lunch and his dinner! Inviting him to stay was the least she could do.

She just wished that the day hadn't been quite so pleasant. Why, the hours had flashed by like lightning! She hadn't been on her guard, as she must always be with Garth, or felt that she was merely pretending to do a job for which she feared she was not truly qualified. She'd actually learned quite a lot today, and she was beginning to feel that she could actually pull this off. Besides all that, she and Dale worked well together. Too well, perhaps.

She reached the parlor to find Hypatia and Magnolia there.

"Hello, dear," Hypatia said with a smile. "You're running a bit late, aren't you?"

Petra nodded, caught her breath and said, "Actually, I've been here for a while, going over some things with Dale, and I'm afraid I've kept him longer than I should have, so would it be all right if we set one more place for dinner tonight?"

The sisters traded glances before Hypatia answered, "For Dale, yes, of course."

"I thought it would be okay since you invited him last time."

"I'm so glad you like him," Hypatia said, smiling brightly. "He's such a nice young man."

"Yes. Yes, he is," Petra agreed, suddenly wary. Did everyone think that she liked him? Well, how could she not, really? He *was* nice. And attractive. And helpful. And exciting in a way she'd never found any other man to be. That didn't mean she was getting romantic ideas, though. Did it? Gulping, she muttered, "I'd better run up and change now."

Dashing back across the foyer, she hurried up the stairs and to her room, where she pulled out a casual pair of jeans and a pretty pink T-shirt trimmed with white lace. Quickly

changing, she rushed to the mirror and applied her favorite
pink lipstick then stood back to take a critical look at herself.

"Nice and slim," he'd said with obvious approval.

She couldn't prevent a spurt of delight at that, no more
than she'd been able to when he'd said it in that matter-of-
fact way of his earlier. Studying her hair next, she wondered
if she should sweep it into a jaunty ponytail or leave it down.
She tried to think if he'd ever shown a preference.

Suddenly, she realized what she was doing, and her eyes
widened in horror. Oh, no. She couldn't let herself think like
this. If she started trying to please some man, she would
lose her focus, and that would mean the sacrifice of all she'd
strived so hard to achieve. No, no, she was a career woman.
She couldn't divide herself between romance and work! She
was a fool to think of Dale Bowen as anything more than a
means to an end.

And yet, she couldn't be that cold and calculating. That
wasn't a Christian attitude. Oh, what was wrong with her?
She had to get on top of these inconvenient feelings and keep
her eyes on the prize. She almost had it within her grasp!
Why, she could be manager of an Anderton hotel within
months and part of the upper echelon of the company before
she was even thirty! It was unheard of, would be an incredible achievement. She would come into her own at last, be a
part of something important and impressive.

Besides, that had to be what God intended. He wouldn't
have let things come this far if she wasn't on the right track.
He wouldn't have shown her the Vail, led her to Anderton,
allowed her proposal to acquire the historic Buffalo Creek
hotel to find favor and sail through the purchase with nary
a hitch if He didn't mean for her to be manager. Right?

She nodded at her image. Right. Okay, then. So she would
mine Dale Bowen's impressive expertise and enjoy his company while doing it, but that was as far as it would go. They'd
both benefit, and when the hotel renovations were complete,

they'd…what? Wave at each other around town? Until she went on to bigger things.

For the first time, that thought left her feeling hollow inside.

To Petra's surprise, Dale talked a lot during dinner, starting with the blessing, which Hypatia again asked him to voice. He sat next to Petra this time, with Kent and Odelia across from them and Magnolia at the foot of the table opposite Hypatia at the head. Without Garth there to hog the limelight, Dale proved to be a delightful dinner guest. He seemed perfectly happy to listen to Odelia gush about her wedding plans and shared funny stories about Garrett with Magnolia, who treated their former gardener almost as if he were her son.

Garrett had spent several years in prison after beating his brutal stepfather, who later had murdered Garrett's poor, abused mother. Magnolia had used all the influence of the Chatam family, and Asher's excellent legal skills, to have Garrett pardoned so he need never fear violating parole. Happily married now with a stepson and thriving business, Garrett continued to be the apple of Magnolia's shrewd eye.

"He's a good man," Dale said in reply to her praise of his friend.

"It takes one to know one," Hypatia decreed.

Dale chuckled. "Thanks. I hope that's true."

Kent asked how Dale's father was getting along. Though semi-retired, as a local pharmacist, Kent must have known when Walton Bowen had been hospitalized and why. Dale expressed some concern.

"The doctor's warned him that he's going to have a heart attack if he doesn't learn to take it easy."

"Hardworking man," Kent intoned with a shake of his head.

"Yes, sir. He is that," Dale agreed. "I try to take as much

off him as he'll allow, but he really needs to step back, at least for a time."

"We'll pray that happens," Magnolia told him.

Dale glanced at Petra before saying, "Thank you, ma'am."

"So," Hypatia moved to change the subject yet again. "How is the hotel project going?"

Clearly, she asked this of Dale. Petra shifted uncomfortably. She hadn't informed her aunts of the change in project management, telling herself they would be troubled about something out of their control. In truth, she couldn't help a certain sense of shame for her part in the matter, though she really couldn't have done anything but obey orders.

Dale, bless him, just smiled and said, "There have been a couple of hiccups, but that's to be expected. Everything will work out fine."

Petra telegraphed guilty gratitude with her eyes, and to her surprise, he reached across and patted her hand under the table, as if to say that he understood. The warmth of his touch radiated up her arm and settled in her heart. She fought the feeling for several long moments before Dale provided her with an opening to broach the subject of the arbitration meeting.

"We're currently involved in a little disagreement with the Buffalo Creek Historical Society," he said mildly.

"Oh, yes," she interjected, leaning forward to address Hypatia. "I know that things are crazy right now, but would it be possible for us to meet with the BCHS here at Chatam House?"

"Of course, dear," Hypatia answered immediately. "So long as it's not the day of the wedding."

"I hope it's much sooner than that," Dale said.

When Magnolia asked what the issues in question were, Dale answered succinctly then went on talking about the hotel, detailing some of the things that he loved best and enjoyed working on most here. For the first time, really, the hotel became more than a stepping stone along her career path for Petra. Dale spoke of it as if it were a living entity, full of grace and comfort and old wisdom. Rather like her aunts.

"They knew how to build to last back then," he opined. "That's what I want to do. Whatever I build, I want it to last the ages. I want some fellow, hundreds of years down the road, to say, 'Wow, they really knew what they were doing, and look how they did it!' He doesn't even have to know my name. I just want him to see and appreciate what I built. Or rebuilt," he added, and everyone laughed.

Petra felt a strange sense of pride in him at that moment, followed swiftly by a crushing self-doubt. What would her legacy be? she wondered. *I helped build the Anderton hotel chain. I had a good job.* Somehow, that just didn't seem enough. Yet what else was there for her? What could there be?

Later, after Dale graciously turned down the offer of tea following the meal, Hypatia charged Petra with seeing out their dinner guest. She strolled side by side with him down one hall and then another to the door at the side of the house, exchanging pleasantries about the food. When they reached that bright yellow door, Dale naturally opened it, because that's what any true gentleman would do. Charmed despite her modern, professional outlook, Petra hesitated. She had spent a long, eventful, oddly pleasant day in his company, but she had no intention of walking out onto the wide stoop beneath the porte cochere with him—until she did it.

As he pulled the door closed behind them, she finally faced the truth that everyone else had already seen. She liked Dale Bowen. A great deal. More than she'd ever liked any other man.

She could only hope that wouldn't lead to trouble.

Chapter Six

They went to stand at the top of steps, softly illuminated by an electric light high overhead and a hot sliver of sun still scorching a dark blue velvet sky at the edge of the horizon.

"Man, it just does not cool off this time of year, does it?" Dale commented.

"And July's a'coming," she noted wistfully.

"Ever notice how cool and comfortable it is inside the hotel?" he asked, turning to face her. "All that marble holds a constant temperature. It helps with the cooling and heating costs, too."

"It's not cool upstairs," she informed him, "except in the penthouse."

"The penthouse unit is separate," he explained. "We'll get the others online as soon as the wiring's done, and I'll push the electrical contractors about that, I promise. Rather, I'll see to it that Jackie pushes them."

She knew who would be doing the pushing. Garth might think he'd removed Dale from the job, but she knew better. Jackie Hernandez had been right. Dale *was* Bowen & Bowen. She couldn't help looking up into that strong, handsome face and feeling deep gratitude.

"Thank you for all your help, Dale."

"Thank you for the dinner invitation," he returned softly, and for a moment, just an instant, she wished that things could be different between them. But it wasn't possible. Was it?

After a moment, he shifted, his gaze sliding away and back to her face. "Maybe I can return the favor sometime," he suggested. "Saturday night, maybe? If you don't already have plans."

Taken off guard, she stumbled over a reply. "Oh. I—I don't... That is, it wouldn't be..." She shook her head. Wise. It wouldn't be at all wise to go out to dinner with Dale Bowen, which made her sudden, fierce longing to do so utterly terrifying. "I can't," she finally managed.

He didn't hide his disappointment. "Some other time then," he said, making it as much a question as a statement.

She stood as still as humanly possible, a slight smile frozen in place, afraid to so much as breathe for fear she'd reply in the affirmative. Looking down, he rocked back on his heels. Then he turned and walked down those few steps. His boots crunched across the gravel of the driveway as he moved toward his truck.

"Good night."

"G-good night," she returned, starting to tremble.

As she watched him climb into the truck, back it out and drive away, she realized that Dale Bowen might well be the most dangerous thing in the world to her right now. If she was not very, very careful, he could lay waste to all her plans. Then where would she be? *Who* would she be?

And yet, she realized bleakly, she needed him back on the project. The sooner the better. She couldn't go running off to him every time a problem cropped up; she needed him on-site as much as possible. Now if only she could somehow convince Garth of that fact—and protect her surprisingly vulnerable heart at the same time.

* * *

As it turned out, Garth did not need much convincing. After Petra informed him about the arbitration meeting with the BCHS, he immediately returned from Colorado. As soon as he glanced over the punch list, he instructed her to bring Dale in on it.

"Way ahead of you," she told him matter-of-factly. "He arranged this meeting with the executive committee of the Buffalo Creek Historical Society."

"More like the Buffalo Creek Hysterical Society," Garth groused. "I suppose Bowen has to be there."

Petra just quirked an eyebrow at him. Garth sighed. "Fine," he snapped. "Such a fun way to spend a Saturday."

She had to fight to keep from rolling her eyes as she began to fill in Garth on Dale's plans, item by item. Afterward, he reluctantly praised Dale's solutions, but Petra cautioned him that several tricky issues remained, and Saturday's meeting proved her entirely correct. Only after long hours of discussion did they come to full agreement.

"Just to reiterate the final point," Tansy Burdett, the BCHS chairperson said, "Mr. Bowen will personally oversee these issues and serve as liaison in all future communications between Anderton Hotels and this society."

"While keeping all parties fully informed," Garth added, looking directly at Dale, who nodded in agreement.

Petra could tell that he didn't like having Dale back in the mix, but he had been surprisingly reasonable. She let out the first easy breath she'd taken all day, sure that all would now be well.

"Then I think we are done here," Tansy decreed, heaving her sturdy body from the chair at the head of the table. The woman sounded as tired as Petra felt, and for good reason. Though approaching eighty years of age, Tansy had ruled the proceedings with an iron hand from the beginning. Dale, however, had patiently and adroitly steered her toward certain helpful conclusions, and Garth, to his credit, had allowed him to do it.

"I must say," one of the other committee members piped up, "that I am encouraged by what we've achieved. The Vail—"

"Anderton Vail," Garth corrected, on his feet.

"The Anderton Vail," the woman said pointedly, "could turn out to be the crown jewel of our historical properties."

"We'll certainly work toward that goal," Dale promised, walking around the table to help her out of her chair.

"Within reason," Garth muttered.

Dale shot him a tight smile. "Absolutely. We do have a budget."

"And a schedule," Garth reminded him.

Acknowledging that with a bow of his head, Dale went to fetch a cane for another elderly lady at the table. Garth caught Petra by the arm and ushered her swiftly into the foyer.

"I hope you're pleased," she began, pitching her voice low.

"Under the circumstances, yes," he said, stepping close and speaking softly. "You were right all along about this. I should've listened. Bowen has the old biddies in the palm of his hand. From now on, use him as you see fit."

Petra didn't much like the sound of that. Yes, she'd thought something along those lines herself, but hearing Garth state so baldly that he considered Dale to be nothing more than a tool irritated her. Dale had smoothed many ruffled feathers for them this day. Still, she did not visibly react. Neither did she step away as instinct warned her to. Instead, she murmured something designed to turn Garth's statement as much in her favor as possible, even if she didn't like herself for it.

"Thank you for that vote of confidence."

"You've earned it," he told her. "Wish I could stay around and watch you in action, but I've got to get back to Colorado."

"I understand."

"Good." He glanced behind her, smiled and slid his hands across her shoulders. The next thing she knew, he was kissing her!

Frozen in shock, she did nothing more than stand there with her eyes wide open and her lips clamped shut.

After a couple seconds, he lifted his head, stepped back and waved nonchalantly at someone behind her, saying loudly, "Thanks for your help on this, Bowen. Ladies, take care."

Petra's face flamed, but she still couldn't seem to move. Several long seconds ticked by before she came to the inescapable conclusion that Garth had staged that kiss for maximum benefit. He'd planned to stake his claim in front of Dale Bowen all along. That, of course, meant that he, like everyone else apparently, realized how attracted she was to Dale. She knew with humiliating certainty that she should have expected something like this from Garth; he'd given in too easily to Dale's involvement. Cringing inwardly, she tried hard not to let her dismay show on the outside, telling herself that at least her aunts hadn't seen that kiss. On the other hand, with Tansy Burdett there to witness it, they might as well have! Still, what was done was done. She'd just have to make the best of it.

Gathering her courage, she cleared her throat and turned around. While she'd been wallowing in humiliation, the foyer had filled with those taking their leave. Not a one of them would meet her eye, and though she wished the floor would open up and swallow her whole, she had to do, say, something. Now. Before it was too late. Dale stood at the door, waiting for the old dear with the cane to clear it. Petra immediately went toward him.

"Dale, if I could—"

"I noticed you were taking notes," he interrupted lightly,

his gaze not quite meeting hers. "I assume you'll be typing those up."

"Y-yes."

"I'd appreciate a copy."

"You can have mine as well," Tansy volunteered, coming up beside Petra.

He smiled at the older woman. "Great. I'd like to have everyone's."

"Very wise," Tansy pronounced, nodding in approval even as she frowned at Petra.

"Well, I guess we're done here," Dale said cheerfully. Now that the doorway had cleared, he nodded to no one in particular and left.

Petra feared for a moment that she might cry, but then she squared her shoulders. This was best, she told herself sternly, at least so far as she and Dale were concerned. Things were getting far too personal between them. Really, she should thank Garth for effectively removing any possibility of a romantic entanglement between herself and the handsome builder. Later, of course, she would put her employer in his place. Meanwhile, neither Dale Bowen nor Garth Anderton could be allowed to throw her off her stride.

She'd searched and searched for an opportunity like this one, and as far as Petra was concerned, she'd just been given carte blanche to see this project through. She'd make the Vail the star in the crown of Anderton Hotels if it was the last thing she ever did. She'd do it if it killed her. She'd do it if it tore out her heart.

But that wasn't going to happen. She wasn't going to *let* it happen.

From now on, no matter what Garth staged, no matter how Dale smiled—or didn't—she was going to become the manager of the Anderton Vail. Then the sky would be her limit. She was going to rocket straight to the top.

All she had to do was keep her wits about her, and she could do that, she promised herself.

Please, God, she prayed desperately, *don't let me mess up.*

If she could just keep her goals in mind, it would all work out. Garth would eventually lose interest and look for easier prey, and Dale... He was a contractor doing a job. That's all. He was a means to an end for her, and she for him. This was business, and there was nothing wrong with that, as long as everyone got a fair shake out of the deal.

If that thought did not bring her the comfort for which she longed, well, that's what church was for, wasn't it? She suddenly couldn't wait for Sunday morning.

"Why, you're as pretty as Walt said," Hallie Bowen told Petra at church the next morning, her cheeks bunching with a wide smile.

They'd met in the foyer, literally walked right into each other. Dale, who had been following close behind his mother, had made the introductions, his smile and tone impersonal. *Which is just as it should be,* Petra told herself, petulantly ignoring the little twist of hurt in her chest.

She thanked Dale's mother for the compliment. "That's a very nice thing to hear. Thank you."

"And who is this lovely young lady?" Mrs. Bowen asked, reaching past Petra to clasp Dallas's hand.

"This is my sister, Dallas," Petra answered, careful to keep her gaze off Dale and on his mother.

Had Dallas not been pestering Petra for details about that kiss Garth had planted on her in the foyer of Chatam House the day before, Petra would not have bumped into Hallie Bowen and she and Dale could have passed with nods and nothing more. Instead, they were standing around making awkward conversation while looking anywhere but at each other.

Hallie Bowen suddenly called out to a young woman across the way, waving her over. "Sudie! Sudie! Over here!"

About Petra's age, the young matron guided one little girl by the hand and carried another on her hip as she made her way across the foyer. The heavy highlights in her short, dark blond hair made her resemblance to Hallie Bowen all the more pronounced.

"Petra," Hallie said enthusiastically as the woman drew near, "this is my daughter, Sudie. Sudie Baker. And these are my granddaughters. Nell is four, and Callie's eighteen months."

Even as her proud grandmother spoke, Callie reached for her uncle. Dale hoisted her easily into the crook of one arm and bent his head to rub noses with her, making her giggle and prompting her sister to claim her share of his attention.

"Hold me, Unca Dale."

"Come on up," he promptly agreed, clasping both of her little hands in one of his.

She literally climbed him, walking up his body as he pulled from above and her mother scolded both of them unconvincingly while brushing down Nell's frothy skirts.

"Nell, you're too big, and you're going to ruin his dress pants. Dale, you spoil them both."

"That's what uncles are for," he said, settling the girl on his hip. "Right?"

"Right!" She stretched up for her nose-rub then sniffed his cheek. "Mmm."

The memory of his aftershave washed over Petra, leaving her weak in the knees—and she hadn't realized that she'd even noted it!

He made goo-goo eyes at the girls and entertained them while Petra chatted with his mother and sister.

"They're adorable girls."

"Thank you. My husband, Don, says they're just like me."

Sudie laughed, while Hallie pointed out all the ways that the girls were like their mother.

"These girls are sweethearts, though," Dale interjected. "Sudie was a mean little thing." He gave Petra the briefest glance, just so she'd know he was teasing, then winked at Nell, who giggled.

Sudie dug her finger into his chest while he laughed. "I was not! I was the best sister ever. I adored my big brother, and you know it."

"You adored biting me," he ribbed.

"I bit you twice. Three times at most!" Sudie exclaimed.

At that, Callie opened her mouth and moved toward either her sister's arm, where it looped about Dale's neck, or Dale's collarbone, exposed by the open neck of his shirt. Sudie snatched her away, complaining, "Now look what you've done."

"Me?" Dale protested, laughing. "I wasn't trying to bite anybody."

"You put the idea in her head."

He leaned down and put his forehead to little Callie's, saying firmly, "No biting. Okay?"

She popped a finger into her mouth and nodded, then she trailed it down his cheek. He turned his head and kissed that tiny fingertip. Petra had to look away, her chest suddenly so tight that it hurt. He had called himself a family man, and obviously he would make a great father. Petra suddenly felt struck by the idea of never being a mother, though she had long ago accepted that such would be the case if she followed through with her plans. Shaken, she tasted a hint of regret.

"We ought to get inside," Hallie Bowen warned as gathering music began to emanate from the sanctuary.

The Bowen family turned toward the tall arched doors, calling farewells. Only then did Petra realize that Walton wasn't with them. She wanted to ask if he was well, but she didn't dare prolong the meeting. Instead, she hung back, smiling and waving until they were through the doors. Even then, she couldn't breathe easily, for no sooner were the Bowens out of sight than Dallas caught her by the crook of the elbow and spun her about.

"Are you crazy?" she demanded, her amber eyes as big as saucers. "You're cheating on Garth with Dale, aren't you?"

Petra's jaw dropped. "*Cheating?* No! For starters, I'm not *with* Garth."

"But you kissed him right in front of—"

"*He* kissed me!" Petra interrupted, fighting to keep her voice low. "I did *not* kiss him, and I've never let him think that I wanted to, either!"

"Well, you'd better start," Dallas warned, "or he's going to get the idea that you like Dale."

"Let him!" Petra snapped, even though she was quite sure that Garth had already gotten that idea. Otherwise, why try to get rid of Dale, and why so obviously stage that kiss?

"You don't mean that," Dallas argued, shaking her bright red curls. "Garth has everything—looks, personality, charm, money…"

"And Dale is what?" Petra hissed, painfully aware that she was more offended than the situation merited. "Chopped liver?"

Gasping, Dallas brought her head up sharply. "You do like him!"

Petra rolled her eyes. "Of course I like him. What's not to like? But it means nothing. Dale and I…get along. Because we have to. In order to work together."

"Then why not see where things go with Garth?"

"I'm just not interested in 'seeing where things go.' Not with Garth or any man."

Dallas folded her arms. "Lying is a sin, you know. And lying in church, well, that's even worse."

She stalked off, her nose in the air. Petra sighed and cupped her hands over her eyes. So much for finding surcease from her problems in church! Good grief. Why couldn't Dallas just leave this alone? If she thought Garth was so special, why didn't she go after him herself?

That thought arrested Petra for a moment, but then she shook her head. Garth was wrong for Dallas for all the reasons that he was wrong for her. He was too much older, too sophisticated, too self-centered and she suspected that he was not a Christian. Dallas needed a strong, solid Christian man who would curb her tendency to meddle. Like Dale.

The very idea of Dallas and Dale chilled Petra all the way to the bone.

Dallas might need someone like Dale, but Dale needed someone like…

Petra couldn't bring anyone to mind. Every time a face or a name slid close to realization, it slid away again. But then she didn't really want to picture him with anyone else. Instead, she pictured him teasing his sister and cuddling his nieces. And barely even looking at her.

Her eyes closed with the weight of the knowledge that, if Dale had ever had an inkling of interest in her, Garth's staged kiss had surely killed it.

And that, she told herself, slowly following her sister, was for the best. Even if it didn't feel like it at the moment.

As for Garth Anderton, she thought grimly, she'd deal with him when he got back to town. She knew from experience that nothing could be done about Dallas, but her meddling sister would realize soon enough that her romantic intrigues were pointless when it came to Petra.

All she and Dale Bowen had going for them was work, and that's all they would ever have.

The amount of work that Dale could get done in a day amazed Petra. He always seemed to be at ease, never rushing or panicking; yet over the next two days, the items on the BCHS punch list began disappearing at an astonishing rate.

Even more incredible, the rewiring of the hotel had been accomplished by late Tuesday, and blessedly cool air now blew from the hotel's air units.

Petra held her hand in front of the wall vent and sighed with relief. "Thank God." Even she had been uncomfortably warm when called upstairs for some reason or another.

"Amen to that," Dale said, moving on down the upper hallway.

They'd spoken countless times since Sunday, but the conversations were always concise and impersonal. Petra missed the easy camaraderie they'd shared before Garth's staged kiss, but she told herself for the umpteenth time that this way was best. Yanking her gaze from Dale's broad-shouldered back, she fixed her gaze on the clipboard that she carried in one hand and wielded her ink pen with the other, checking off one more item and moving on to the next.

"How are we coming with the shower retrofits?" she asked, following blindly along behind Dale.

"Ordered the materials this morning," he replied.

"Oh, good. You found a supplier, then." She made a check mark on her list and picked up her speed. "How about—" She yelped as she stumbled and went down, twisting as she fell so that she landed hard on her rump, clipboard and ink pen flying. "Ow!"

An ominous tearing sound told her that her chili-pepper-red skirt had just been reduced to dusting rags. Maybe she could use it to clean the white dust that billowed up around her, making her cough. She tried to beat it out of her crisp white blouse with one hand while using the other to shift herself out of whatever she'd fallen into. It looked like a heap of broken, pulverized gypsum board or plaster, mixed with bits of lumber and other materials.

Suddenly, Dale was on one knee before her. "You okay?"

"Yeah, I think so. Just give me a minute."

He ran his hands lightly over her shoulders in a soothing gesture. "Didn't you see that pile of debris?"

"No, I didn't."

"Whenever you're ready, I'll help you up. Don't try to stand on your own."

"Okay, but…" She rolled her weight slightly, testing, and grimaced. "I, um, think I'm going to have a problem with my skirt."

His eyebrows rose, and he slid his puzzled gaze over the slender garment. "What sort of problem?"

Petra felt her face heat. "A, um, ripping problem. From the hem to the waistband, maybe."

Comprehension dawned in his green eyes. "Oh! Uh, we can take care of that. Sort of. Here." He started unbuttoning the plaid shirt that he wore over a simple white T-shirt. Shrugging out of it, he rolled down the sleeves and looped the garment behind her, tying the sleeves at her waist in front, so that the shirt would hang down like an apron worn backward. "Okay?"

"Yes. Thank you." The cotton shirt felt soft and silky from many washings and as warm as a blanket. She wanted to bend over and stick her nose into the cuff to see if it smelled of him.

"No problem. Now let's get you up."

She nodded. He moved to her side then took her arm and wrapped it around his neck. Next, he slid his arm about her waist. She tried not to inhale his aftershave or register the incredible heat that seemed always to radiate from him.

"Here we go."

He rose swiftly but smoothly. It was only then that she realized she'd lost a shoe, a red leather flat with a pointy toe and gold buckle.

"Ow, ow. Not good," she sang, her foot protesting any attempt to put weight on it. "Feels like I twisted my ankle."

"Guess there's only one thing to do then," he said, bending to sweep her off her feet. She gasped and threw her arms around his neck. When he straightened, he had her shoe in the hand of the arm supporting her knees. "Want this?"

Her heart had vaulted into her throat. She swallowed it down and said, "Thanks." Taking the shoe, she cradled it against her chest as he started forward, carrying her down the hall toward the elevator.

She felt oddly treasured and almost smiled, catching herself only at the last instant. Still, she couldn't stop herself from exulting in the warm strength of his arms. She wanted to lay her head on his strong shoulder and just be the weaker vessel for a little while. Something told her, perversely, that she could find strength in that, but she couldn't let herself believe it, not while she rode helplessly in his arms. Not when she wanted so desperately to be right where she was.

Chapter Seven

Lifting her leg, Petra made a show of frowning at her ankle. It had already started to swell.

"Think it's broken?" he asked.

"Hope not. Don't think so. I didn't feel that kind of pain."

"We'll get an X-ray to be sure," he said, as if that settled the matter.

She didn't argue. She was too distracted by the feeling of being in his arms.

They reached the elevator, and he carried her onto it. "You'll probably want to hit the button."

"Shouldn't you put me down first?" she asked reluctantly.

"I'd just have to pick you up again," he said, maneuvering so he could poke the lobby button with his elbow. He held her tight while the elevator jolted into motion then lowered to the ground floor. All the while, she babbled in an effort to keep unwise delight at bay.

"I—I feel like such a fool. I should have watched where I was going. Was that stuff even there when we came by earlier? I don't know what I was thinking."

"Accidents happen," he said as the elevator came to rest.

She couldn't think what to say to that. Being held by him

felt so good, so right, and even though he radiated heat like a campfire, she didn't feel burned. She felt…safe.

Suddenly her ankle started throbbing like a big bass drum. She tried worriedly to wiggle her toes, and managed it. Sort of. That didn't give her any comfort.

"Maybe it is broken."

"We'll soon find out," he told her, carrying her across the lobby.

A trio of workmen came through a door just then and stopped in their tracks.

"Boss?" one of them queried worriedly.

Dale kept walking. "Little accident. Nothing serious. Get on about your business. Tell Jackie that Miss Chatam and I are gone for the day. And get someone to clean up that debris in the hallway on the third floor!"

"Yes, sir."

They were on the sidewalk before the three men had scattered.

"My car's in the hotel lot around the side of the building," she informed him.

"Mine's right here," he replied, carrying her to the white double-cab truck parked at the curb. "Hold on."

He put a foot on the running board, and effectively balanced her on his knee while he fished his key from his pocket and opened the door. The backseat, she noticed, was stacked neatly with plans, notebooks and others papers. He eased her inside, buckled her safety belt as if she were a child and walked around the front of the truck to slide behind the steering wheel.

"There's a primary care clinic a few blocks from here."

"Maybe I should head home to change first," Petra began, but he cut her off.

"Nope. X-ray first. Then home."

Petra sighed. She knew he was right, but she didn't have to like showing up with his shirt tied around her waist.

When they arrived at the clinic, he parked the truck and went inside, returning a few moments later with a wheelchair. After settling her, he pushed her into the building. Half an hour later, she got that X-ray. An hour after that, they were still waiting for the doctor to come speak to them. During all that time, Dale stayed by her side, chatting about one thing or another, the job, his nieces and sister, his dad, who had felt unwell on Sunday morning and been convinced to sleep in.

"Probably in the same fashion I was convinced to have my ankle x-rayed before going home to change," Petra mused grumpily. Dale laughed.

"It was something along those lines. Quit grousing. So your skirt got torn. You're decently covered."

"I hurt," she complained, and she did, from her ankle to her waist. But at the same time, she was deeply grateful for Dale's calm, commanding presence.

"I know you do," he told her, patting her hand. "Won't be long now." And it wasn't. The doctor came in a few moments later.

The ankle was not broken, thankfully. After receiving a brace and instructions on how to apply ice packs and deal with the sprain, Petra was given a sample of a mild pain reliever and discharged.

"Where am I going to get a crutch?" she worried aloud as Dale put her back into the truck.

"Well, I'd bet Kent can help you there."

She brightened instantly. "Of course!"

"Now let's get you home."

Pandemonium reigned for several minutes after Dale carried Petra through the front door and into Chatam House, surprising Odelia, who nearly swooned as she was coming down the staircase. He thanked God that she didn't, for how he'd have seen to her with Petra in his arms, he couldn't imagine. Odelia's squawk brought Kent, who never seemed to be far away, running from the library, followed by Hypatia and Magnolia, both of whom came from the front parlor. For a while, everyone asked questions at once, with Petra trying to reassure one only to break away and answer another. Finally, Dale took charge.

"She's fine!" he announced, raising his voice. When the chaos subsided, he explained further. "She took a little fall and twisted her ankle, but it's not broken. Still, she has to stay off it. Kent, she's going to need a crutch."

"Yes. Yes, of course." The round fellow took off at a trot.

"Ladies, we need ice packs. The doctor suggested bags of frozen vegetables."

"As if Hilda would use anything but fresh," Hypatia sniffed, sounding almost affronted.

"Then baggies of crushed ice," he said, disciplining a smile as he moved toward the staircase. "She's going to need help getting undressed and comfortable, too," he went on.

"I'll see to that," Hypatia volunteered, falling in behind him.

"I'll crush the ice," Magnolia announced grimly.

"She'll need tea," Odelia decided, her hands fluttering anxiously, "and treats. Oh, I hope Hilda has ginger muffins."

Dale looked down in time to see Petra bite her lip against a smile. He cleared his throat of laughter and started climbing.

"Are you sure you can manage on your own?" Hypatia asked Dale anxiously.

"She's not heavy," he replied.

Oh, he could manage to carry her upstairs, all right. The question was, could he manage to let go of her once her got her there? He didn't want to. That much was certain.

He wondered what he was going to do about her. Garth Anderton obviously wanted her, and Garth had everything going for him. Maybe Garth was what she wanted, too. He'd seen that kiss, after all. In fact, he'd relived that moment a thousand times since. Once he got past the feeling that some-one had driven a white-hot poker through his chest, though, he'd started to remember details, like how she'd stood stock still, her arms stiff at her sides, while Garth had kissed her. Her head hadn't even moved. That might have meant that she didn't like Anderton's kiss, or that she simply didn't go for public displays.

Dale reminded himself that even if she wasn't involved with Anderton, she wouldn't necessarily want anything to do with him, either. They didn't have much in common, after all. He was a simple man doing a simple job that revolved around the family business, and she was a career woman on a fast track, not a housewife like his mom and sister. Shiny as new gold, she dressed as if she belonged in the penthouse, not the upstairs apartment of his folks' old place. But he had to find out if he might have a chance with her anyway.

Okay, God, he thought, *any advice?*

God did not, as was His habit, immediately answer. For once, Dale wished He would.

They reached the landing, and Hypatia bustled ahead to open the door to Petra's room. Dale carried her inside and deposited her in the corner of the pale purple brocade sofa, careful to protect her ankle. Hypatia hurried off to fetch something comfortable for her to wear, while Dale stood there like a bump on a log staring down at her. She looked tiny and fragile and achingly beautiful with her hair coming down and his shirt tied around her waist.

As if his thought reminded her, she began picking at the knot in the sleeves, saying, "Oh, you'll be wanting this."

"No, you keep it," he said automatically.

She said nothing to that, just looked up at him with those big, warm honey eyes of hers. Then she reached out her hand. He folded his own around it, clasped it tight.

"Thank you," she whispered.

Just that, and he suddenly had a lump the size of Kansas in his throat. Bending at the waist, he placed a light kiss on her forehead and got out of there. Still, he couldn't make himself leave the house. He thought about going to work in the suite, but he didn't want to take a chance on disturbing Petra, so he went downstairs and let Odelia ply him with tea until Hypatia came down and reported that Petra was sleeping comfortably.

"We'll launder your shirt for you, dear," Hypatia said, "as soon as she's done with it."

A picture of Petra sleeping in his shirt flashed though Dale's mind. He had no reason to think that was happening, but it was a sweet image. Finally, he rose to leave. He very much feared, as he drove away, that he was leaving behind more than just his old shirt.

After a strangely sleepless night, with his restless mind chasing one subject after another down myriad blind alleys, Dale headed back to Chatam House early the next morning. He fairly crept up the stairs, fearful of disturbing a sleeping Petra, only to find her limping toward him with the aid of a single crutch. She'd left her hair down, pushing it back from her face with a hard plastic headband the same shade of teal-green as the wide-legged pants and matching jacket that she wore with a brightly patterned scarf.

"Surely you're not going to work!" he protested.

"Of course I'm going to work," she told him. "Why wouldn't I? It's just a little sprain."

He could have argued with that, but he knew from the look on her face just how much good that would do him. Besides, if their positions were reversed, he'd likely do the same thing. That didn't mean he approved.

"Give me that," he said, practically yanking the crutch from her hand, "and lean on me."

She slipped her slender arm up and around his neck without argument, which went a long way toward mollifying him. He helped her hop down the first two steps, but then he stooped to wrap an arm about her waist and simply straightened again, lifting her off her feet. With her dangling like a human necktie, he ran down the steps with her. She laughed, and the sound of it made him ridiculously happy. He thought of his nieces and the fun that they always had together. Those moments of uncomplicated joy were the closest he'd come to this feeling.

He kept right on going until they reached his truck.

"I shouldn't let you drive me," she said, "but my car's still at the hotel."

"Well, then," he countered, settling her inside the cab, "good thing I happened along when I did."

"You always seem to be around when I need you," she remarked softly, stopping his heart inside his chest. He fought the crazy impulse to tell her that he would always be there for her, but of course, he could make no such promise so he said nothing all, reaching for her safety belt. She lightly slapped his hand, scolding dryly, "I'm not helpless."

He backed off, mentally shaking his head at himself, and jogged around to slide behind the steering wheel. She could buckle her own safety belt, for pity's sake. They were well on their way to the hotel before he trusted himself to speak.

"Sleep well?" he asked.

"So-so. Lots of aches. You?"

He shrugged. "Had a good deal on my mind."

"Oh. Your dad?"

"Partly."

"How is he?"

Dale sighed. "Working on the payroll. We had office staff to do that, but we had to cut back."

"Ah."

"Better than having him in the field, I guess."

She nodded. "I always find numbers soothing."

"Really? I like working with numbers, too. That's a big part of construction. It's paperwork I can't stand."

She laughed. "I'm far better with paperwork than a measuring tape."

"Yeah, I'd guess so."

"To each his own, as they say."

"Right," he agreed. "We all have our contributions to make."

Once they reached the hotel, she insisted on making it inside on her own. He watched her hobble along, following behind until he saw her safely ensconced behind her desk in her office. She gave him a knowing smile.

"You can go nursemaid your father now. I'll be fine."

He chuckled. "Actually, I need to work at Chatam House today if that's okay."

"No problem, but if you're coming back around lunchtime," she began suggestively, "I think Hilda could be persuaded to find something for us to eat."

He grinned, ridiculously pleased. "See you then."

Smiling, she shooed him away with a wave of her hand. He went out laughing, but he knew that he wouldn't be able to stay away for long, not until she felt fully recovered. And probably not even then.

Picnic basket in hand, Dale walked back into the hotel at fifteen minutes past eleven. Predictably, Hilda had leapt at the opportunity to provide them with a feast. Petra looked up from the calculator she was pecking numbers into and smiled.

"You're early. I thought you would be Dexter coming back to harangue me about the lobby furniture. Again."

The prissy decorator tended to flit around in his oversized shirts, funky shorts and flip-flops, but the guy had good taste. He could be exhausting, however, just through the sheer force of his personality.

Petra propped her swollen foot on the seat of a chair that someone had dragged up to the desk for her and applied an ice pack that Hilda had sent along, while Dale laid out the luncheon, complete with china plates and linen napkins. They ate and chatted, about the hotel mostly. Petra seemed bright and determined, but he could tell that she was flagging.

"Are you sure you're not ready to go home now?" he asked as he packed up the remains of the meal.

"I'm fine here," she assured him, but he noted the blue tinge under her eyes and determined to return shortly to check on her. He did so more than once, finding excuses to pop in every hour or so.

It made for an awkward day, running back and forth between Chatam House and the hotel, but by twenty minutes past three, Petra seemed so obviously exhausted that he scooped her up, giving her no chance to protest, and carried her out to the truck. She glared at him, grumbling that she was "not a baby" and "capable of making her own decisions." He didn't argue, but he did take her back to Chatam House, where she insisted on climbing the stairs on her own.

She managed well enough, with the aid of the crutch and the banister, until her cell phone rang. Leaning against the wall, she dug the tiny device out of a pocket and lifted it to her ear.

"Oh, Garth," she said, and Dale's hackles instantly rose.

He tried not to listen to the conversation, something about the lobby furniture, and watched her for signs of physical instability instead. After a few minutes, she began to sag. Then her crutch slipped away, clattering down the steps. Of course, she made a grab for it, wincing when her bad foot touched the step and nearly toppling over in the process. Dale had had enough.

Without a word, he swept her up into his arms again. She

gave out a tiny squeak and glared at him, but went on with the conversation doggedly.

"You're arguing with the wrong person," she told her boss. "Dexter is the one who has to be made to see reason."

The tinny sound of Garth's raised voice made Dale want to hurl the phone to the marble floor below. Fortunately, his hands were full at the moment. Still, he took the stairs two at a time and got to the top as quickly as possible. When he reached the door to her room, he managed the knob himself and simply carried her inside, where he plopped her down on the brocade sofa, her back to the arm as before. She was still trying to reason with Anderton.

"Dexter claims that he can make up the cost. I've looked at the numbers myself, and—"

Something came over Dale. Something primal and male and irresistible. He reached down and snatched the phone out of her hand, lifting it to his own ear.

"Has Petra told you about her accident?" he demanded, ignoring her gasp of outrage.

Utter silence followed, then, "What accident? And who is this?"

"Give me that!" Petra hissed, making a swipe at the phone.

Dale stepped back out of her reach, saying, "She took a fall yesterday and sprained an ankle bad enough to be on crutches now. And you know who this is."

He could almost hear Garth Anderton's blood boiling, but to the man's credit, he didn't let his temper get the better of him. "Is she all right?"

"Bruised, sore, exhausted and in some pain, but she'll mend, especially if she stays out of the office for a few days, which she seems disinclined to do. I physically removed her from the premises earlier."

Anderton steamed for a moment, then Dale heard a gulp. He couldn't help enjoying the other man's predicament.

That's what he got for planting that kiss on her in such a public place.

"Tell her I'll call Dexter and get this issue settled," Anderton finally ground out.

"Will do," Dale replied cheerily before shutting off the call.

He offered the phone to Petra, and she nearly took his hand off when she grabbed it away from him.

"How dare you?" she seethed. "You had no right to—"

"Someone had to tell him that you've injured yourself, and you obviously weren't going to," he growled back at her, beginning to see that he'd overstepped. Badly.

"That's my business! Not yours!"

The fact that she was entirely correct made it all the worse. He sighed. "I know, I know, but I couldn't just stand by and let you pretend that everything is okay."

"I'll *pretend* if I want!" she snapped. "I've worked too hard and too long to get this far and now you're messing it all up for me!"

He suddenly felt lower than a snake. "Right. Sorry. Don't know what came over me."

"You don't know how many ways I've tried, how many paths I've taken," she went on in a shaky voice, "and this is the first thing that has panned out, my first real chance at…" Tears spilled from her eyes, each one a tiny dagger into his heart. "S-success," she gasped before clapping a hand over her quivering lips.

His heart dropped like stone, as did the rest of him. He found himself sitting on the corner of the coffee table just behind him and reaching for her. To his vast relief, she let him take her hands.

"Hey, now," he said, soothingly. "Garth won't blame you. I commandeered your phone and poked my nose into your business. He's bound to realize that, and if he doesn't, then I'll make sure he understands."

She shook her head and choked out, "No, thank you. You've done quite enough."

"Pet, I'm sorry," he said urgently. "I didn't think. I—"

"What did you call me?" she demanded, suddenly spearing him with her amber gaze.

He blinked at her, uncertain. "I, um…"

"My grandfather used to call me Pet," she said softly.

Dale realized suddenly that he'd been calling her that in his head for some time now. He swallowed and searched for something innocuous to say. "You were fond of your grandfather?"

"He used to pat my head and call me his little Pet and tell me that he loved me," she said, sniffing.

"That's nice," Dale said lamely.

"He told me how my name meant 'rock' in Greek and that it is the rock of faith upon which the church is built."

"Yes."

"And he said it was a name that would make me strong," she rattled on shakily, "and I've tried so hard to be, but I—I've failed so often already, and I don't know what I'll do if this doesn't work out!"

Dale leaned forward and gathered her into his arms, his heart breaking for her. "Here, now, sweetheart," he crooned. "You're as strong a woman as I've ever known. You're just tired and hurting right now. That's all this is."

"I *am* tired," she said on a little gasp. "I'm tired of failing! If I can just get this project in on schedule and budget…"

Dale felt his chest tighten. "You will," he promised. "I'll help you."

"You already have," she told him, drawing away with a sniff. "I'm sorry I snapped at you."

"I'm sorry I stuck my nose into your business," he said. "I didn't realize how important this job is to you."

"It's my chance," she told him, her hands curling into fists, "my one chance to finally make it."

"I don't understand how that can be. If this doesn't work out the way you hope, you can always try something else."

"But that's what I've been doing," she protested, "and in my family, that's not how it works."

Truly baffled, he let his hands drop to his knees. "You'll have to explain that."

She made a face. "You probably know that both of my parents are doctors."

He hadn't known, and he shook his head. "Go on."

"And there's Asher," she went on, "a lawyer, a very good one."

"You don't have to tell me," Dale said. His family had trusted Asher Chatam to handle their legal affairs for several years now.

"And Phillip," Petra went on. "That's my other brother, with his grand adventures, mountain climbing and such. We can't even find him half the time."

Dale frowned. "Sounds dangerous," he said. Not to mention thoughtless, possibly even selfish.

"But it's his passion!" Petra exclaimed. "That's the point. In my family, everyone has a passion, a calling, a *career*. Even Dallas, the baby of the family, knew she wanted to be a teacher before she graduated high school. But me…" Petra sighed and looked down. "I've just never known where I belonged. In this whole family of overachievers, I'm the one failure."

"Now that's silly," Dale told her.

"No, it's not," she insisted. "Everyone has a career but me."

"Maybe you're not meant to have a career," he pointed out. "That doesn't make you a failure. My mom has never worked outside our home, and my sister did only briefly."

Petra didn't seem to even hear him. "I've prayed and prayed about what to do with my life," she confessed raggedly, "and when I found this, I thought…well, this is my chance."

"Listen," he argued gently, "if this doesn't work out, that doesn't mean you're a failure. You don't have to have some stellar or glamorous career to be a success. You're only a failure if you let someone else's definition of success keep you from finding your real heart's desire. Once your find that and you lay it at God's feet, He'll help you do and be all that is necessary."

"That's exactly what I am doing," she stated firmly. Then she gave him a false smile, adding, "I won't keep you any longer. I'm sure you have things to do. Thank you for bringing me home. I'll send Chester for my car later, so you won't have to worry about providing me with transportation anymore."

"I don't mind," he began, but she cut him off.

"I am *sooo* tired," she said, slumping back on the couch. "As soon as you're out the door, I'm going to have a nap."

He rose at once, knowing that he couldn't do anything then but go. Several heartbeats passed before his feet obeyed his mind, however.

"Take care of yourself," he murmured, moving away. His last sight of her before he pulled the door closed troubled him. She looked so lovely and wounded and alone. That was exactly how he felt as he padded down the stairs.

Alone.

Chapter Eight

Petra stayed home from church that evening. She felt guilty about it; she'd gone to work that morning, after all, but she couldn't seem to face the prospect of midweek services. Dale would be there, and she couldn't see him again. Not yet. Never before had she confessed her misgivings to another soul, and she wished mightily that she hadn't done so this time. She'd just been so tired and achy that she'd lost her temper when he'd informed Garth of her injury. Then one thing had led to another, and suddenly she'd been pouring out her heart to him. Now she was more confused than ever, and the things he'd said kept running through her mind.

"Maybe you're not meant to have a career. That doesn't make you a failure."

What did it make her, then? She couldn't find a label for a woman who'd held a succession of mid-level jobs in varying fields.

The aunts looked in on her before they left, carrying away the barely touched dinner tray that Hilda had sent up and generally fussing over her as if they had nothing better to do, while she knew perfectly well that the whole house was abuzz with preparations for the wedding.

"Now, you just rest, dear," Odelia said, patting her hand.

"And call downstairs if you need anything," Magnolia added.

"We'll say a prayer for you tonight," Hypatia told her as she followed the other two from the room.

Petra sighed. She hoped they'd pray for her miserable, messed-up life in addition to her miserable, aching ankle. She hoped they'd ask God to send her instructions and plans addressed specifically to her and preferably carved in stone, thank you very much. She couldn't stop thinking about Dale and about what he'd said to her that afternoon.

"You don't have to have some stellar or glamorous career to be a success."

But how could that be? From infancy, her parents had drummed into her the importance of having a goal, a plan. They believed that God called everyone to something, and He seemed to have done just that with her brothers and sister. Why not her?

"You're only a failure if you let someone else's definition of success keep you from finding your real heart's desire."

But that was the problem. She didn't have a "real heart's desire." She only had Anderton Hotels.

Petra wanted to believe that Anderton Hotels was her calling, but how could she be certain? Confused and weary—everything was twice as difficult with crutches and a sore ankle—she struggled into nightclothes and lay upon the bed, her gaze caught by the freshly laundered shirt hanging from a hook on the bathroom door. She swallowed a couple of analgesics and prepared herself for sleep, but she found herself praying, instead, on all sorts of topics: Odelia and Kent, Asher and Ellie, her brother Phillip out in Seattle, her sister Dallas, things at the hotel, her career, her parents, Walt Bowen, Garth, politics, world peace…everything except what truly troubled her.

Yet somehow she heard, if not an answer, then at least a *suggestion* concerning her dilemma. Maybe it was time to talk to someone who just might understand, someone whose judgment she trusted implicitly. So when Hypatia came in to check on her before bed, as Petra had somehow known she would, Petra was ready.

"Can we talk?" Petra asked. "I'm so confused."

"Of course, dear," Hypatia answered, drawing an armchair to the side of the bed. She wasn't surprised. She had known that something serious was afoot from the moment she'd caught sight of Dale Bowen's troubled expression as he'd stalked across the foyer that afternoon, oblivious to everything and everyone around him. "What is bothering you?"

Petra explained haltingly but in great detail what was on her mind.

Hypatia listened attentively, secretly surprised by what she heard. Gathering her thoughts, she bowed her head for a moment's silent prayer and began to try to alleviate her niece's confusion.

"Strictly speaking, dear, I suppose they are all right—Dale and your parents."

"But how can that be?" Petra protested.

"Well, I believe that God does call us all to serve Him, sometimes with one overarching purpose, sometimes with many purposes and in many ways. I believe that the mother whose singular focus is keeping her home and caring for her family is as called as the preacher who fills the pulpit on Sunday or the doctor who treats the ill." Hypatia smiled with self-deprecating humor. "Or the old maid who doles out her dollars and sits on committees."

Petra gasped. "Oh! I didn't mean to imply that you or the other aunties are any less…" She bit her lip, the words trailing off.

Hypatia patted her hand. "I know you didn't. I also know that your mother has never understood my sisters and I. Partly, I suppose, it's a generational thing. Far fewer careers were open to women when I was your age, but I don't think it would have mattered."

She could tell by the look on Petra's face that she didn't understand, so Hypatia settled in to try to explain, sitting on the side of the bed.

"I've never had any need to earn a living, but once I realized I wouldn't marry, I expected that God would call me into the mission field in some way. I dreaded it, frankly," Hypatia admitted sheepishly, "and as the years slipped by I began to fear that I wasn't listening as well as I should have been. Eventually, however, I realized that I was exactly where I was supposed to be, doing exactly what I was supposed to be doing."

"Why didn't you marry?" Petra asked softly.

Hypatia shrugged. "I just wasn't interested. I don't know why, but I could never see myself as someone's wife or mother. I've been quite content as a daughter, sister and aunt."

"I've heard people say that perhaps the time is past when people ought to be thinking of marriage and children," Petra ventured uncertainly.

"Oh, I don't think so," Hypatia disagreed. "I dare say that in some quarters marriage has lost its cachet. So many people seem to find it passé, old-fashioned, unnecessary, and that has not, in my opinion, been good for our society."

"Yes," Petra agreed, "but obviously marriage isn't for everyone. I mean, it's difficult to have a career and raise a family, too."

"Difficult—but not impossible," Hypatia said. "Just look at your own parents."

"Well, that's what I mean," Petra told her. "You don't know how often as a child I wished my mother would just come home."

Hypatia chuckled. "I'm sure all children feel that way at one time or another, but I can't criticize either of your parents, Petra. Just look how well you and your siblings turned out!"

Petra frowned. "But I haven't really accomplished anything yet."

Shocked, Hypatia blinked at her. "How can you say that? You're a lovely young woman, and you've had some wonderful jobs."

"Yes, but those jobs went nowhere."

"Where did they have to go?" Hypatia asked, confused. Petra just stared at her. Hypatia patted her hand again. "You're young yet. Give yourself a chance to see what God is doing in your life."

Petra sighed. "I just want to know where I belong, what I'm supposed to be doing."

"We all want that, dear, even when we don't realize that's what we're after."

"I guess," Petra muttered.

"Now can I ask you something?" Hypatia ventured.

"Of course."

"Is everything all right with you and Dale?"

Petra started. "Me and Dale? Why would you ask that?"

"Well, I couldn't help noticing how concerned he's been for you, and he seemed rather troubled this afternoon. I just wondered…" She shrugged, confiding gently, "I heard about Mr. Anderton and that kiss, you know, and I couldn't help thinking that Dale must have been…hurt."

"No!" Petra said. Then her brow furrowed. "Do you think so?"

"He seems to like you," Hypatia offered obliquely. "Of course, so does Mr. Anderton."

Petra didn't seem to be listening any longer. She sat up in bed, drawing up her knees and wrapping her arms around them, her gaze targeted on something across the room. Hypatia followed her line of sight, smiling when she saw Dale's shirt hanging from a hook on the back of the bathroom door.

"I'll let you rest now," Hypatia told her, rising to go. She paused to suggest, "You know, you might want to study the thirty-first chapter of Proverbs. It might give you a little insight."

"Oh?" Petra muttered absently.

"I think it would be very helpful," Hypatia told her, bending to place a kiss on her niece's pale head.

"Thank you," the girl returned vaguely. Hypatia left her to her thoughts.

Sighing silently, Petra dredged up the extra patience that she needed to deal with her boss these days.

"Period materials and techniques are expensive, no doubt about it," she said into the mouthpiece of her office phone, "but we'll make it up on the back end, and we have a bit of room now." Because Dexter had decided that reproductions were more serviceable than genuine antiques, the budget had gained a little weight. "Besides, I have a surprise for you," she went on.

"It had better be good," Garth grumbled. He'd complained about the construction budget, but Petra knew he was more concerned about the expense being incurred in Colorado, as well as the time away from the Vail project.

"The BCHS has agreed to include the hotel in this year's annual Yesterday's Christmas event," she divulged proudly. "It's a big deal here, Garth. All the historical buildings in town vie for the chance to participate, but only half a dozen are chosen each year. We'll need to decorate in period style, lavishly, but people come from all over to take the tours, busloads of them. The Cracked Crock Café got national reviews when they were included."

"Okay," he said. "I'm impressed."

"But there's more," she went on. "A local reporter from a Dallas TV station has agreed to do a piece on the hotel once it's open for business. He brought up an interesting question, though. He wanted to know if we would be reopening the pool in the basement. Apparently, it was put in sometime during the 1920s, so I think the BCHS would be okay with it. I have the guys looking into it, and if the pool's viable, we won't have to go to the extra expense of building a new one."

"Well, you are just brimming with good news and bright ideas," Garth praised. "How's your ankle, by the way?"

"Better," she said. "Don't worry about me. I'm fine."

"Great. I look forward to seeing you when I get back to Texas."

"I look forward to seeing you, too," she returned dryly, thinking that she was going to finally put him in his place about that kiss.

They hung up, and she glanced up to find Dale standing in her office doorway. Obviously, he'd been there for several moments and had heard her say she was looking forward to seeing Garth again. Dale did that finger-down-the-nose thing.

"Think you can make it downstairs? I need you to take a look at the pool."

She pushed back her chair and started to reach for her crutch, but stopped. Her ankle had improved, and the crutch had become more trouble than it was worth. Before she could decide whether to try to walk without it, Dale sauntered over and presented his elbow.

"Can I lend you an arm?"

She smiled at that. "Sure. Beats that torture device known as a crutch," she told him, hobbling along at his side. He chuckled, keeping his pace slow.

"Well, you won't need it much longer."

"My ankle is better."

When they reached the elevator, he pushed the button for the basement, and the elevator began to drop. Mere seconds later, they stepped out into the darkened underbelly of the building.

"We're going to need overhead lights," Dale pointed out, "quite a few of them. As for the pool…" He offered his arm again.

She leaned against him and limped forward to the edge of the enormous rectangular hole in the center of the floor. The space had been boarded over at some point in the past, but Dale's crew had removed the covering to expose the pool. She couldn't tell much about it until Dale reached over and clicked on a work lamp atop a tripod. Then she gasped.

"Oh, my word! It's beautiful!"

"And in decent shape," he reported. "Some of the decorative tiles will have to be replaced, and we'll need new drains and a modern filtration system, but I really think it's going to take a minimal amount of work to get it approved and open."

"That's wonderful news!"

"There's more," he told her. Turning, he waved a hand at the many doors and rooms behind them. "Were you aware that there was a spa down here?"

"A spa?"

Nodding, he ticked off what he'd found behind the doors of what everyone had taken for ample storage rooms. "Mud baths, his and her saunas, exercise room, massage beds. We even found a barber chair and some sort of Medusa-like curling-iron thing, so I think we can safely assume that they had a barbershop and beauty salon at some point. And these other rooms…" He turned to gesture toward the far wall. "You might want to think about turning them into shops."

"That's brilliant!" she exclaimed. "But will the BCHS go for it?"

"Maybe, if we can prove that such services were offered on-site in the past. I'll see what they say."

"This could work out so well!" she enthused. "Garth's been concerned because Buffalo Creek is so far from the downtown business centers of Dallas and Fort Worth, but a spa would give us something else unique to offer. Like his-and-her spa packages! What do you think?"

He shrugged. "Yeah, I guess."

"Oh, come on," she teased, whacking him playfully on the arm with her hand. "Wouldn't you go for a couple's weekend spa deal? Think about it. While she's getting a facial, body wrap, hairstyling and chemical peel, you could go for a nice haircut, old-fashioned shave and a good workout followed by a sauna, swim and massage. And then a romantic dinner in our restaurant."

"Sounds like fun," he said, snagging her gaze with his, "*if* I was part of a couple."

In the blink of an eye, the atmosphere changed. Petra's breath caught.

"Are you part of a couple, Petra?" he asked softly.

She couldn't decide if she should answer lightly or make a firm statement of denial because she could neither read nor escape the intensity of those leaf-green eyes. She settled for a simple shake of her head.

"No? It's obvious that Anderton's interest in you goes way beyond business," Dale said. "How serious is it between the two of you?"

Petra warred with herself, fearing that she was about to step onto a dangerous path, but she couldn't bring herself to lie to him.

"There's nothing personal between Garth and me," she managed, "nothing at all. That kiss you saw was the first and only. And not exactly a mutual idea."

A small, tight smile curved Dale's lips. "That kiss did look a little…"

"Staged," she finished for him, surprised by how relieved she was that he'd noticed her lack of participation.

His smile widened. "I wonder why he'd stage something like that?"

Petra gave a little shrug that she hoped appeared appropriately nonchalant. "You can never tell what goes through Garth's head."

"I somehow got the idea that he likes to weed out the competition," Dale said, "if you know what I mean."

She knew what he meant, and he knew that she knew what he meant, but she tried for an unconcerned tone anyway. "I suppose."

"Maybe," Dale said, stepping closer, "you need something to compare Garth's kiss with. In the spirit of competition."

Stunned, Petra looked up. Oh, dear! He was going to kiss her. What should she do? But she already knew what she was going to do—and that it would change everything. For ill or good, nothing would be the same after this. Still, she couldn't have stopped him if she'd wanted to—and she did not want to stop him.

When he stepped closer still, she placed a hand on his chest and looked up into his eyes. He slipped an arm around her waist and cupped her cheek with the other hand. Pressing his thumb gently beneath her chin, he tilted up her face. As he lowered his head, she leaned in and stretched up to meet him, her arms sliding up around his neck.

The room whirled. For a moment, she thought it was her, that she must surely be falling, but then she realized that both of her feet were firmly planted on solid ground. The ache in her ankle proved it. The fact that she barely noticed the pain proved just how lost to sanity she was.

The instant their lips met, Dale knew that he had just done a very foolish thing. This kiss, unlike any other he had known, threatened to rob him of his good sense and set him on the path of stubborn self-rationalization. He had no business kissing this woman. Everything he knew about her proclaimed that she was not for him. Still, from the moment he'd first laid eyes on her, Dale had not been able to get Petra

Chatam out of his head. When they were together, she felt so right, as if the cogs and wheels that made her work somehow meshed perfectly with his, as if God had designed her for him alone. But how could that be when they were so different? Was it possible that a successful career woman from one of the area's foremost families could be the woman God had chosen for him, the son of a blue-collar family with no pretensions? Dale knew only that he had to find out.

With aching deliberateness, he began pulling back incrementally until he'd broken the kiss and put almost a foot of space between them. He stared down at her beautiful face. She looked as stunned as he felt, her amber eyes slightly glazed. That made him smile. So much about her made him smile.

Clearing his throat, he backed up another step, his hands at her waist, steadying her. She blinked and blew a breath upward, while he racked his mind for something intelligent to say. The only thing that came to mind was, *"Wow,"* but he managed to keep the word behind his teeth. She seemed to have heard it, nonetheless, for her eyebrows leapt in tandem before settling back into place. He desperately sought the next step, but he couldn't quite think what that ought to be. Dropping his hands, he put a bit more distance between them, and his mind began to clear.

She was not the sort of woman he'd ever thought he'd want because he wasn't at all sure she would put marriage and family before career, and Dale very much wanted to be married and make a family of his own. He'd just been waiting for God to bring the right lady along. How could that be Petra, though? She saw things through the spectrum of career and business, while he saw them through the prism of marriage and family.

Looking at it logically, Garth Anderton was a better match for her. They had ambition and the hotel in common, and given her family's emphasis on achievement, Garth's success in business must make him very attractive, indeed. Just the idea of her and Garth together had been eating Dale alive, though! He couldn't shake the feeling that he had to try with her. He had to know if she might be the one for him and vice versa.

Lord, help me, he prayed automatically, and then his mouth kicked into gear. "Uh, we should… That is…" Suddenly he knew what they should do. "My mom would be delighted if you'd join the family for dinner on Sunday after church." Yes, that would do. That would do very well.

Petra looked confused for a moment. "Are you asking me out?"

Dale squared his shoulders. "Yes. I'm asking you to join me and my family for Sunday dinner."

Her brow furrowed, and she dropped her gaze to the floor. "Why?"

Why? He cleared his throat. "That kiss ought to tell you why."

He wasn't going to find out if they could have a future together by kissing her, though. Kisses like that would do nothing but muddle his brain, when they both needed to find out if they could fit into each other's lives.

For a long, awful moment, he thought she would refuse his invitation, but then she looked up again and simply nodded her head. He let out a breath that he hadn't realized he'd been holding, and his brain finally began functioning at full speed again.

"Want to meet at church? Or should I pick you up after?" he asked.

She took a deep breath, coughed behind her fist and swallowed. "Meet."

He didn't know whether to dance a jig or brace himself for eventual disappointment, so he just stood there like a bump on a log. "Okay."

They stared at each other for several seconds longer, until

she wobbled slightly. "Oh. Here." He quickly stepped to her side, offering his arm.

She smiled wanly and slid her hand around the crook of his arm. "So inconvenient," she said softly, referring to her temporary lameness.

"I don't mind," he told her.

Mind? If he'd been a little less wise, he'd have hauled her into his arms and carried her again.

They inched their way back to the elevator then rode in silence up to the lobby. He walked her to her office and saw her settled comfortably in her chair, her bad ankle propped up on an overturned box with a fresh ice pack applied.

"Can I get you anything else?" he asked.

She shook her head. "No. Thank you. And Chester is coming to drive me home."

He nodded, thinking that was probably a good thing. "Well," he said, "if I don't see you before, then I guess I'll see you Sunday."

"Sunday," she echoed.

He tore himself away and headed straight out to his truck. When he got there, he bowed his head and closed his eyes. *Am I being a complete fool?* he asked his Lord. *Or is it possible that she really is the one?*

He didn't know what to think anymore, but he knew that Sunday would not come soon enough.

Chapter Nine

Sunday seemed forever away to Petra. No matter how often she told herself that she was being foolish, she couldn't help feeling excited about spending Sunday afternoon with Dale and his family. Neither could she help reliving that kiss.

It could not have been more different from Garth's. His kiss had stunned and irritated her; beyond that, she didn't really remember much else. Dale's kiss, on the other hand… She had no words to describe it, no context in which to place it, but she couldn't forget a second of it, and that made no sense to her. Nothing about her feelings for Dale Bowen made any sense.

Dating anyone wasn't part of the plan. She couldn't afford to be sidetracked or distracted, but since Dale had kissed her, she couldn't seem to care about the danger to her career. Not yet. She thought long and hard about it, and decided that sanity would return in due course. Meanwhile, she might as well enjoy being crazy. At least that's what she told herself when Dale popped into her office on Friday afternoon to chat about some information he'd garnered from the BCHS historian.

"She seems to recall that the Vail was once touted as a 'businessman's health resort' and suggested that we check out the old editions of the local newspapers to see if we can find mention of it."

"And if we do, the BCHS will okay a new spa?" Petra asked.

"Provided the renovations and décor are period-correct."

"That's great news!"

"Want a ride to the library and an extra hand?" he asked. "They have old newspapers on microfiche."

Petra grabbed her purse from her desk drawer. "That's quaint. I thought everything was computerized now."

"Small-town libraries have small-town budgets," he pointed out, waiting while she got to her feet and clomped over to the door in her flats and brace.

They drove the few blocks to the library in his truck. Like everything else in Buffalo Creek, the building held historical significance, starting with its Greek Revival façade. Petra had to take the stairs up to the intricately carved doors slowly, but Dale showed great patience, pacing her carefully in case she should fall. Inside, he took charge, speaking to the surprisingly young woman behind the information desk. Within minutes, they were seated side by side at twin viewing desks with microfiche reels loaded in the viewers.

At Dale's suggestion, they started in the early 1940s and worked their way backward, pausing from time to time to read aloud interesting headlines and even whole stories. They laughed about sales ads for products that hadn't existed in decades and old political cartoons. Finally, Petra came across an article dated February 10, 1938. The author reported on a new "strengthening treatment" now being offered at "our lauded and very popular local health spa beneath the fine Vail Hotel." The article went on to claim that the spa at the Vail was known in business circles as far away as New York City and San Francisco.

Excited by this reference, Petra began combing through newspaper editions from the previous era. Dale found references to the spa in several editions of another newspaper, the oldest going back to 1919.

"Well, this ought to satisfy the BCHS!" Petra exclaimed as they waited for copies of the articles to be made.

"And score some brownie points with the boss," Dale pointed out.

Petra kept to herself the fact that she'd already blown that opportunity. Garth had seemed seriously pleased when she'd informed him about the possibilities of the spa, but she'd felt honor bound to tell him that he could thank Dale for the discovery. She'd then listened to Garth gnash his teeth on the other end of the telephone connection before he'd growled something about needing to confer with "a real contractor" and hung up.

"I'm less concerned with scoring points with the boss than the BCHS," she told Dale truthfully, a little surprised that it was so.

"Why don't you put together a presentation," he suggested, "and I'll set up a meeting with the executive council."

"I could do that," she mused, imagining a slide show and a list of talking points. Dexter would help with the conceptual end of a proposal.

"Why don't we stage this one at the hotel?" Dale asked. "We'll show them around the place, let them see our progress and lay out our plans."

Petra beamed. "That's a wonderful idea!"

"You're going to get that promotion yet," he said, tapping the cleft in her chin.

Thanks to you, she thought, *and the good Lord, who brought you to me.*

"We should celebrate," Dale heard himself say as they retraced their steps back to his truck. He felt flush with success, though in truth he had little to gain from this new project unless Garth agreed to pony up additional money, which didn't seem likely. Dale couldn't resist the opportunity to see Petra smile, however, and he wanted to make up for getting her into hot water with Garth the day that he'd taken her phone.

To his surprise, she smiled and asked, "What do you have in mind?"

He immediately pictured a dim restaurant and a candlelit dinner for two and started thinking about a good place to go on a Friday night. Then he remembered that he already had an engagement tonight. Disappointed, he decided to ask her to come along. No one would mind.

"Ever been bowling?" She stopped, lifted her eyebrows and pointedly looked down at the brace on her ankle. He smacked the heel of his hand against his forehead and immediately started apologizing. "Sorry. I forgot! It's just that we have this sort of unofficial team thing going on once a month at the local alley."

She burst out laughing. "I'd be happy to pass the evening as an observer, if no one minds."

"We can always use a scorekeeper," he told her, grinning.

"I can do that."

"Okay, then."

He walked her to the truck, helped her climb up inside and drove her to Chatam House. "Want to go back to the hotel or home to Chatam House?"

She checked her watch. "Might as well head home, save Chester the trip."

"Home it is."

He stopped the truck in front of the dignified antebellum mansion a few minutes later, then got out and went around to help her alight.

"I'll pick you up about seven, if that's all right."

"I'll be ready."

Dale wondered if he would be. So much for waiting until Sunday dinner with his folks! Still, it wouldn't hurt to introduce her to his friends. He'd just keep things casual until he saw what developed—and pray that what developed wasn't a giant heartache.

Before dinner with the aunties, Petra changed into jeans and a bright green, sleeveless, knit top with a high neck in front and a back that dipped several inches. She caught her hair into a loose ponytail at her nape and let tendrils float about her face, hoping that the brace on her foot and ankle didn't lay waste to her efforts.

Waiting by the front window in the foyer, she saw Dale's truck as soon as it turned off the street onto the drive. Quickly, she bade the aunties good-night and limped out onto the porch without the aid of the now-hated crutch. She'd told them only that she was going out with friends, lest they get ideas about her and Dale—ideas that she was trying very hard not to get herself.

She made it all the way to the bottom of the porch steps by the time Dale brought the truck to a halt. He hopped out, ran around and almost put her into the front seat before trotting back around to slide onto the driver's seat. Wearing snug, dark jeans and a simple blue T-shirt, he was in high spirits.

"Looking good," he said, sweeping her with his gaze.

"What?" she teased. "You thought I'd be all buttoned down like I am at work?"

"Is that what you call it?"

"What do you call it?"

"Classy," he said automatically.

She laughed, delighted. "And I'm *not* classy now?"

"Too classy for a bowling alley," he returned smoothly, "but let 'em eat their hearts out."

She laughed again. "Thanks."

When they got to the alley, he grabbed a ball bag and shoes from the backseat then came around to help her out.

She walked into the building on his arm, although she could have managed well enough on her own.

Two couples and another guy were holding the lane for them. She knew Garrett Willows, the former gardener at Chatam House, and his wife, Jessa, the florist for Odelia's wedding. She had also done Asher and Ellie's flowers. Dale's sister, Sudie, was there, too. She introduced her husband, Don, a stocky fellow with outrageous dimples.

Dale introduced Larry Colbert, a tall, thin man with startling blue eyes. He had a rather dour look about him, but Petra soon learned that, in this case, looks were deceiving. Larry cracked a joke every ten seconds and generally kept everyone laughing all night long. His wife, Jeannie, worked at the grill in the bowling alley. Tall, with long dark hair, she'd wander over every so often and drop off something for them to eat.

Garrett and Dale tied for second place, with Don bringing up the rear. Sudie and Jessa played against each other, Sudie winning handily.

Don jokingly offered Petra, the official scorekeeper, a bribe of cheese fries to bump us his score.

"Uh-uh," Dale objected good-naturedly. "My date cheats for me and nobody else." He winked at Petra, who felt a broad smile spread across her face.

"Oh, I always cheat *for* my date, never *on* him," she quipped.

"That's my girl!" he exclaimed, taking up his ball again. Petra couldn't help feeling a thrill at his words, though she told herself not to be a ninny. She wasn't "his" girl or anyone else's.

After two games, during which Larry admittedly "smoked 'em," Jeannie walked over and sat down, while the guys bowled a third game. The Colberts left, Jeannie complaining that she was exhausted after Larry won the third one in a row. Dale, Don and Garrett played one more game, with

Dale winning by a whisker. Don did even worse than before, but if he cared a fig about his score, Petra couldn't tell it. He was there to have fun, and with Larry gone, he became the cut-up.

At the end of the evening, while everyone but Petra changed into street shoes, Garrett invited anyone interested to accompany him and Jessa to the local Renaissance Festival a week from Saturday. Petra noted wistfully that she hadn't been to the annual festival in at least a decade.

"I've never been," Jessa confided, sounding excited about her first time.

"It'll be the first Saturday afternoon we've taken off since we opened Willow Tree Place," Garrett said.

"And the last until after the wedding," Jessa put in.

Sudie made a face and said, regretfully, that she'd agreed to help her mother-in-law with a garage sale.

"Which means I'll be babysitting," Don declared happily.

"If sitting in a recliner watching baseball on TV is babysitting," Sudie drawled, to much laughter.

To Petra's surprise, Dale raised a brow at her and asked, "Want to go? Your ankle should be fine by then, but if not, we could get a wheelchair for you."

"A wheelchair at a Renaissance Festival?" she said, shaking her head. "I don't think so."

"Actually, they have wagons made of wood that we can pull you around in," Garrett informed her.

"I think I can manage for an afternoon," she decided impulsively.

Dale beamed. "Great! We'll go in our own vehicle so we can leave anytime you want."

"Sounds like a plan," Garrett said.

It occurred to Petra as Dale drove her back to Chatam House that they were actually dating now. One date did not constitute "dating," but a date with a second and third already planned, well, that couldn't be called anything *but* dating.

She wondered again what she was doing. But then she told herself that it was just bowling, a Sunday dinner and an afternoon at the Renaissance Festival, after all. It wasn't as if they were going steady, or whatever the adult version of that might be. Besides, she owed Dale for coming up with the spa idea and helping her sell it to the BCHS. The fact that she enjoyed his company was just a bonus.

A huge, scary bonus.

When he helped her into his truck once more, she thanked him without quite meeting his gaze.

"I just want to be sure you're up to dinner on Sunday," he teased. "My mom would be deeply disappointed if you had to cancel."

"I'm fine," she assured him.

"Glad to hear it," he told her softly, chucking her under the chin.

Her gaze snagged on his, and for a moment, she thought he might kiss her again, but then he backed away and closed the door before heading around to the driver's side. She didn't know whether to be disappointed or relieved, but she had a difficult time sleeping that night because she couldn't stop thinking about Dale or how much she enjoyed being with him. Only after spending a long time in prayer did she finally drift off, right in the midst of, "Please don't let me forget my goals."

Petra had expected the aunties to question her about her date on Saturday, but they were too consumed with details of the coming wedding to do more than make passing comments.

"I'm glad you finally got out of the house," Odelia said before holding up a magazine photo of an enormous hat.

"You don't think this is too much for a maid of honor, do you?"

Since the maid of honor in question, Hypatia, hated hats, Petra quickly formulated an appropriate reply. "It's so lovely, I'm afraid it would upstage the bride."

Odelia quickly turned the page, hat forgotten.

"I hope you had fun," Hypatia said, gratitude shining in her amber eyes.

"I did. Thank you. I haven't been bowling since I was in college."

Magnolia looked up at that. "Garrett was going bowling last night. I stayed with Hunter so he and Jessa could have the evening out."

"Yes," Petra said lightly. "I saw them there."

"That boy will be calling him Dad long before the adoption is final," Magnolia predicted.

When Petra said nothing to that, Hypatia spoke up. "And did you see Dale?" she asked innocently.

Petra wasn't about to lie to them. "Of course." With that, she quickly excused herself. She'd thought the matter closed until she came downstairs the next morning.

Petra had chosen a simple cotton dress to wear to church and dinner afterward. Sky-blue with yellow, green and white flowers, it sported a square neckline, fitted bodice and full skirt that fell well below her knees. Abandoning the ankle brace, she chose white sandals and left her hair down, pinning back the sides with pearly barrettes. Upon first sight of her, Odelia offered the loan of a pair of daisy chain earrings. Knowing her aunt's penchant for oversized jewelry, Petra politely declined. Hypatia supported her by citing Dale's young niece, Callie.

"So tempting for little hands," she pointed out, indicating a complete knowledge of Petra's plans.

Odelia, clad in pink gingham, a white straw hat and pink

ice earrings the size of jewel boxes, clapped her hands. "How lovely! You're seeing Dale again today!"

Stunned, Petra managed a polite smile. "As a matter of fact, I'm having dinner with the Bowens after church."

"You'll certainly fare better at Hallie Bowen's table than ours on a Sunday," Magnolia pointed out.

The aunties "ate simple" on Sundays, doing for themselves so that the staff didn't have to work on the Sabbath. In keeping with that tradition, Kent would be driving the town car to church that morning.

He tooted the horn after bringing the car around to the front of the house. Hypatia winced, but Odelia ran for the front door with a happy smile. Magnolia and Hypatia followed more sedately. As the youngest, Petra went last.

Before he handed her down into the backseat, Kent remarked, "Odelia has a lovely pair of earrings to compliment that frock, my dear."

Petra glanced at his red-and-white candy-cane-striped vest and couldn't help smiling. No wonder he adored Odelia so. They were a matched pair.

"So she mentioned. I'll keep that in mind for next time," Petra told him.

In no obvious hurry, Kent tooled along the city streets in the long town car while Petra fought the urge to check her watch. The minutes had never seemed to pass so slowly. When Kent let them out in front of Downtown Bible Church, across the square from the hotel, Hypatia and Magnolia immediately began climbing the steps to the tall, heavy doors, but Odelia elected to wait at the curb for Kent. Petra forced herself to stay with Odelia until Kent parked the car and crossed the street to join them. Only then did she take herself off to her own Bible class.

After what felt like an interminable hour, Petra was surprised but pleased to find Dale waiting for her when the class let out. "Hello," she said with a smile.

"Hello yourself," he said, sweeping her with his gaze. "You look like a perfect summer day."

Thrilled, she smiled and flipped a finger at a single pearl stud in one earlobe. "You don't think daisy chains would improve my ensemble?"

"Daisy chains?"

She laughed. "Aunt Odelia offered me a pair of earrings to complement my dress."

"And you wisely declined them," he commented, hastily adding, "I mean, I'm sure they'd look lovely on your aunt, but on you I prefer a style that's more—"

"Dainty," she supplied.

"Classy," he amended. He'd described her as classy before, and she quite liked the idea.

"Thank you."

He was looking quite classy himself in dark dress slacks, a short-sleeved, olive-green pullover of some silky knit and ostrich skin boots. Somehow, his bronze-and-gold hair managed to appear neatly combed and charmingly rumpled at the same time. His leaf-green eyes smiled at her, and Petra felt it all the way to her heart.

Dale explained that it would be simpler if they sat together during the service rather than try to find each other afterward. He had a point. The sanctuary aisles tended to clog for long minutes after the service.

They joined his family, Hypatia nodding approvingly from the Chatam pew further down the aisle. The Bowens gave her a warm welcome, making ample room for her and asking about her ankle. She assured them she was fine then blushed when Dale said, "Don't worry. I won't let her overdo," as if she was his to protect.

For the first time, Petra wondered what it would be like to have a man actually look out for her, care about her.

After church, she and Dale got into his truck and followed the rest of his family in Sudie's minivan to the Bowen

house on the south side of town. The Bowens all lived together in a large, two-story home, older but definitely not
on the historic register. Sheathed in white siding, it sported
a deep front porch and green metal hip roof. A covered
stairway, with a landing halfway up, led from the drive in
front of the freestanding garage to a doorway on the second
floor. That, Dale informed her, led to his private apartment
upstairs. His parents lived downstairs. Sudie, Don and the
girls all had upstairs bedrooms but shared living space with
his parents.

Hallie went straight to the kitchen and put on an apron
over her church clothes, trading her dress shoes for house
slippers. Walt trudged off to change out of his suit while Don
disappeared with the girls and Hallie put Sudie and Petra to
work.

"The dishes to lay the table are in the cabinet in the dining
room," she said to Petra, pointing the way with a wood
spoon. "Napkins and flatware are in the drawer on the right
side. Sudie can get down the glasses and fill them."

Dale winked at Petra as she went dutifully to lay out the
china. She gave him a little shrug, and he went off smiling,
reappearing in the dining room minutes later wearing jeans
and casual boots with that silky T-shirt.

As he watched her fold white dinner napkins to lay beside
the periwinkle china, he further explained the living arrangements. "Don and Sudie have the original master suite. Mom
and Dad converted the downstairs den for themselves, and
there's an extra room for guests. I even have an extra bedroom in my apartment and my own kitchen. They don't get
used much, though."

Petra sniffed the air, aromatic with pot roast. "I can see
why."

"Seems a waste to cook for myself when Mom and Sudie
are down here cooking for everyone else," he said.

His nieces ran into the room just then, dressed in play clothes. "Swing us, Unca Dale! Swing us inna tree!"

"After dinner," he promised. "Maybe Dad will let you watch TV until then."

"Yeah, thanks!" Don called from the living room. "The game's on."

"Donnie Baker!" Sudie shouted from the kitchen. "Let your daughters watch a little TV, and I have news for you. We're watching a movie after dinner."

Don groaned, while Walt advised, "I'm taping the game. We'll watch it later."

Dale chuckled. "Typical Sunday at the Bowen/Baker house."

Petra smiled. It all felt terribly comfortable and homey, almost familiar in a wistful way, which made no sense at all. Sundays in her parents' house were days of near silence with everyone decompressing from a busy week after church. Petra longed for a little of that silence now, a chance to center herself and regain her perspective. At the same time, she sensed a closeness among the Bowens that called to her and made her feel a little sad.

"Dale, the roast!" Hallie called.

"Mom needs me to get the roasting pan out of the oven," he told Petra. "She'll be making gravy next, and then we'll eat."

"Better get this table done then," Petra said, shooing him off with a wave of a hand.

His green gaze held hers for a moment longer, then he hurried away. Petra looked around at the wainscoted room with its old-fashioned flowered wallpaper above the painted bead board and the tarnished brass of the light sconces on the wall and marveled that these people were happy, truly happy, here. Somehow, it didn't feel like enough, and yet when she saw Don and Sudie together or

Dale looking at her with those glowing green eyes, she felt such a fierce longing that it frightened her.

Don and Walt got to see a little of the baseball game after dinner, while Dale took the girls upstairs to play for a bit, and Sudie and Petra helped Hallie clean up after a tasty, traditional dinner of pot roast, potatoes, green beans, cabbage and carrots. Then Sudie put the girls down for naps, and Don queued up the movie. Surprisingly, it was an action flick that the guys all liked. Walt and Don occupied identical recliners, while Hallie claimed an upholstered rocker that sat in front of the fireplace, and Sudie draped herself across an overstuffed armchair in a corner. That left the couch for Dale and Petra.

Dale plopped down in the center and stretched out a long arm across the back, crossing his legs so one ankle balanced atop the opposite knee. Petra sat primly beside him until he slid to the corner and suggested that she kick off her sandals and put up her feet to prevent swelling in her ankle. The ankle was a bit puffy still, so she scooted over next to him and turned to lift her bare feet onto the cushions. His arm just naturally dropped down to cradle her against his side. The movie ended for Petra at that point. Compared to that arm holding her snugly and the shoulder against which she pillowed her head, everything else was just background noise.

The rational part of her brain told her that she should get up and run as fast as she could, lest all her plans be destroyed, but her heart kept whispering, *"What if...what if... what if you could have a career and this, too?"*

Chapter Ten

A s soon as the credits started rolling, his mother launched out of her chair. "Who wants peach cobbler?"

Dale mentally sighed. He'd have preferred to sit right where he was with Petra snuggled against him, but his dad and brother-in-law already had their hands in the air, and he heard sounds of movement from the girls upstairs. While Sudie moved toward the staircase tucked into the hallway behind the dining room, Don started scrolling through the DVR list in search of his ball game. The idyll had ended.

Might as well have cobbler.

"I'll have a bowl, Mama," Dale said, looking to Petra as she swung her feet down to the floor.

"Not me, Mrs. Bowen," she said regretfully. "I'm still stuffed from dinner."

Sudie returned with the girls and plopped Callie down in her father's lap, while she went off with Nell, returning moments later with huge bowls of steaming peach cobbler topped with melting ice cream. Don fed Callie from his bowl, while she lounged sleepily against him and Sudie shared with Nell, who seemed mainly interested in the ice cream. Dale sat back and enjoyed himself.

"Sure you don't want some?" he asked Petra.

"I'll explode if I do, and I can't imagine where you're putting it. I have never seen anyone eat as much as you."

"And stay so thin," Don complained.

"Pound some nails, you'll slim down," Sudie commented.

"What? You saying I'm losing my girlish figure?" Don teased, patting his mounded middle.

"No, honey," Sudie shot back. "Why, you look just like I did when I was pregnant with Callie."

Dale laughed. "You asked for that one, bro."

Petra shook her head, smiling at their antics.

As soon as he polished off his dessert, Walt closed his eyes and, predictably, went to sleep in his chair. Heedless of his father-in-law napping beside him, Don shouted encouragement to his team. Walt never stirred.

Hallie bustled back into the room with a glass of iced tea in hand. "These girls need to get outside for a while," she declared.

Dale volunteered to take them out to the backyard, hoping Petra would accompany him for a few minutes of relative privacy. Encouraged when she slid her feet into her sandals, he deflated again when she offered to take his dessert bowl to the kitchen. Handing it over, he tried to tell her with his eyes that he'd like her to join him.

He needn't have worried. He'd helped Nell into the swing that dangled from the limb of the oak tree that sheltered the play area and was making sure that the sandbox was safe for Callie when Petra slipped out the back door and came to ask what he was doing. After plopping Callie down on her bottom and handing her a tiny plastic shovel, he straightened and tossed aside the large, slotted spoon he'd been using.

"We sieve the sand to be sure nothing's gotten into it."

"Oh," Petra said. "Like what?"

"Scorpions, lizards. Squirrels sometimes bury acorns in there. They go right into the mouth."

"Ugh," Petra said, frowning down at Callie.

Dale chuckled. "All kids put things in their mouths until they learn better."

"I've never heard that," she replied slowly, "and my mother's a pediatrician, but then I've never really been around many kids."

"Your mother's a pediatrician and you've never been around kids?" he asked in surprise.

Petra shrugged. "Not really. I mean, other than my brothers and sister."

"Don't any of your friends have kids?"

She gave him the oddest look. "I suppose some of them must. I just…haven't kept up very well."

He tried not to let his dismay show. He'd known, of course, that she was focused on her career, but not even to know if her friends had children! Did she even have friends? he wondered. He repositioned a pair of painted metal lawn chairs that his mother and sister used when watching the kids while they played. Waving Petra toward one of them, he went to push Nell again before settling down in the other chair.

"You must think I'm awful," Petra commented softly.

"No, I don't think you're awful," he told her. "I do think you've missed out on a lot."

Just then, Callie sent sand flying, sprinkling her hair and pelting Dale and Petra.

Embarrassed, Dale hurried to correct her. "No, no, don't throw it." Leaning forward, he propped up the plastic pail that went with the spade. "Fill that. It's all empty. Look. It needs to be filled." Callie complacently began dumping sand into the little bucket.

Nell cried, "Push me, Unca Dale!"

He twisted around and reached back just in time to connect the palm of his hand with the soles of her feet as she swung forward, giving her a mighty shove in the opposite direction.

"Whee!"

When he turned back to settle into his chair again, he saw that Petra was grinning. "What?"

"You're just so good with them," she said.

He smiled, pleased. "I've been with them since they were born."

"I don't know if I could do what you do," she told him with a shake of her head.

"Watch the kids, you mean?"

"I mean all of it," she said, spreading her hands. "I can't imagine living in the same house with my family now. We all went our separate ways and never looked back."

"That's not true," Dale refuted. "You see Asher and Dallas fairly often, don't you?"

"Yes, of course, but we don't live together."

"Well, I won't always live with my folks, either. One of these days, after I marry, I'll build my own house. This house will go to Sudie and Don, and in return we'll never have to worry that Mom and Dad won't have a place or be cared for when the time comes that they can't care for themselves. Meanwhile, why should I live alone elsewhere when the people I love best are here? It's not like there isn't room or I don't have any privacy."

"I see." She thought for a minute then haltingly said, "When my family did all live together, the best times were Wednesday evenings. My parents worked half days on Wednesday, unless there was a real emergency. We kids would come home from school, and the help would all be gone, and Mom and Dad would be there. We'd go out to dinner and then to church. We had a rule about no TV on Wednesdays, so we'd play games or just sit around and talk."

"You say 'the help' like it's a normal, everyday thing to have staff around the house," he noted, frowning at this proof of the differences in their lives.

"For us, it was," she said, "but not on Wednesdays or Sundays. After church on Sunday was a quiet time for us, but Wednesdays were really all about talk."

"What did you talk about?" Dale asked idly, sensing that she wanted to tell him.

"Lots of things," she said, "but mostly about the future. Asher would say he was going to play professional soccer or maybe be a lawyer."

"We know which goal he went after," Dale noted.

She nodded. "Phillip would talk about Mount Everest and Sir Edmund Hillary. He'd name all the highest peaks in the world and talk about designing gear so he could climb them."

"Interesting."

"And Dallas," Petra went on, rolling her eyes. "All she ever wanted to do when we were kids was play school."

"Of course, she was always the teacher," Dale surmised, smiling.

Petra nodded. Then she sighed. "And me...I was all over the place. Never could settle on a single goal. One week it was dancing and theater. The next it was the stock market. One time I became enamored of working on a cruise ship. Later, I got it into my head that I wanted to coach college-level volleyball. Then I lost interest in the sport and didn't even go out for the team the next year. That's the way it's been my whole life," she complained miserably. "My parents despaired of me. They even had me tested for Attention Deficit Disorder!"

"Oh, Pet," Dale said, taking her hand in his. "Don't you know that the vast majority of the world is just like you?"

"Not you. You've always known what you would do," she pointed out.

"Honey, if my family was in meat processing, I'd be a butcher!" he told her. "Most of the world thinks in term of *jobs,* not career. We just want to keep the bills paid and food on the table. Most of those don't even care how they do it, so long as it's honest work and not too dangerous or stressful."

"My parents have always stressed the importance of finding your passion," she said.

"That's because they're passionate about their own work," Dale pointed out. "They'd have to be in order to be doctors, and there's nothing wrong with that, but it doesn't mean that everyone has to *work* at their passion. My grandma has a passion for ceramic figurines. Her house is stuffed with them. But she worked in a dry cleaner most of her life. My grandpa was a meter reader, and the only passion in his life is *Grandma*. They're two of the happiest people I know."

Petra shook her head. "If you only knew how many different jobs I've had!"

"But you didn't get fired from any of them, did you?" he asked pointedly.

"No, of course not. I just realized I didn't like what I was doing or that the advancement opportunities were nonexistent. A few times, I left because something that seemed more promising came along."

"That tells me you're a capable, desirable employee," he said, squeezing her hand. "I already know you're an excellent manager."

"How can you say that," she demanded, "when you've bailed me out so many times?"

He fixed a level look on her. "Ninety percent of solving a problem is knowing where to find the solutions. And you didn't even let your egotistical, overbearing boss keep you from coming to me when you knew I had the answers. That's what I call good management. I don't know why you are so determined to call it failure."

She stared at him for a good ten seconds. "Oh," she said. "I never thought of it like that."

"Well, start thinking of it like that," he advised.

Just then, he realized that Nell was calling him. He got up to go to her. Callie also stood—and promptly fell face forward into the sand. She howled as if she'd been shot. Dale yanked her up and plopped her down again in Petra's lap, swiping at her sandy face as he turned toward Nell, who was trying to climb out of the safety swing. He got Nell out of the hard, rubber shell seat and turned back toward Callie in time to see her literally spit sand in Petra's face. He closed his eyes.

Oh, that was all this day needed. He'd be surprised if Petra would even speak to him after that. He reminded himself that they had a date for the Renaissance Fair on Saturday and wondered just how soon she'd call it off. Well, the sooner the better, he supposed, before he lost his heart completely.

Her afternoon with the Bowen family gave Petra lots to ponder. She had to consider that she might have been concentrating on the wrong thing, namely her so-called career, to the exclusion of more important matters, like her family and friends. Even worse, she feared that she'd failed some important test. It should be obvious to Dale by now that she was the least domestic woman on the face of the earth.

Petra hated to admit even to herself that she'd never cooked a full meal, never cared for an elderly grandparent, never even changed a diaper! When Dale had dropped his wailing, dirty little niece in her lap, Petra hadn't had the foggiest idea what to do. She hadn't even realized that the child's mouth was full of sand—until Callie had spit it at her. No wonder the poor baby had cried!

Dale had seemed uncharacteristically subdued after that, and Petra had felt a certain sense of panic about it, which was why she had impulsively proposed on the drive home that they take the girls to the park. Dale actually stammered in shock.

"The p-park? Really? When?"

"How about Wednesday?" she'd heard herself say. That, after all, had been the best day of the week when she'd been growing up at home with her parents.

"You mean, like, during the day?" he'd asked. "Because they go to sleep right after church on Wednesday evening."

"Lunch!" she'd proposed brightly, thinking that Hilda wouldn't mind packing a picnic for them.

And that was how she wound up waiting on the sidewalk in front of the hotel on what had to be the hottest day of the summer thus far. She'd had sense enough to wear a light brown pantsuit and comfortable flat shoes, her hair caught in a spiky knot at the nape of her neck—but the perspiration misting her skin belied her cool, calm appearance.

Dale pulled up to the curb, not in his double-cab truck but in Sudie's minivan, with the girls belted into safety seats in the back. Petra lugged the picnic basket that Hilda had packed for them that morning over to the van and said hello to the girls while Dale stowed their meal behind the driver's seat. The girls looked right through her, their attention focused on the basket. Petra walked around and let herself into the passenger side. Dale drove them to the Chataugua Park. There Dale and the girls chased around the graveled playground and climbed over the jungle gym in the ninety-plus heat, until a little boy about five years old joined them. Displaced by the newcomer in Nell's eyes, Dale carried Callie over to the shaded table from where Petra watched the action.

She'd covered the table with a checked cloth and laid out plastic containers of food. Dale dropped down beside her, the baby on his lap, and peeked under the lids, stealing a hard-boiled egg and gobbling down half of it before sharing the rest with Callie. They had slices of cold chicken and green beans to offer her, too, along with crackers and a bowl each of strawberries and grapes.

Dale fixed a plate for Nell, then called her over and parked her next to Petra before carrying Callie around the table to the other bench. Nell dove into her food with both hands before Petra could manage to clean them with the antibacterial wipes that Hilda had included. Dale just chuckled.

"I've seen these kids eat out of the dog's bowl. She'll live."

Petra cleaned Nell's hands anyway. She didn't want the girls getting sick on her watch.

After she'd eaten, Callie became drowsy. Dale cuddled her against his chest and patted her back until she drifted off to sleep, while Nell "helped" Petra repack the picnic basket, turning over one dish in the process and stepping on the lid of another. She ran off to play as soon as Petra closed the lid on the basket.

Dale turned his back to the table so he could watch Nell as she played. Petra walked around and sat down beside him. He smiled with what looked like utter contentment. He was happy, Petra realized, truly happy. This was the life he wanted, the life he would have with whatever woman he would choose for a wife and the children they would have together. This was his world, and he wanted no other. She wasn't sure that it was a world she could inhabit on a daily basis. How did a career woman fit into the Bowen/Baker domestic scene?

"Can I ask you something?" she said.

He removed his aviator-style sunglasses, wiped his forehead with his wrist and smiled down on her. "Sure."

"You said your mother never worked outside the home, right?"

"Never," he confirmed, sliding the dark glasses back into place.

"And your sister only worked for a short while?"

"She helped out at the office until she got pregnant with Nell."

"I see. What does Don do?"

"He's a mechanic, works at a local auto dealership."

"And they live with your parents because…"

He pressed the glasses to the bridge of his nose then swept his finger down the length of it. "That's the way everyone likes it. Same with me. No sense paying rent elsewhere when Mom and Dad can use the money."

"I imagine the rent is quite reasonable, too," Petra said, smiling in case he'd thought she was criticizing.

"Very. And once the mortgage on the house is paid off, Dad can afford to retire."

"He's young for that, isn't he?"

"Fifty-four," Dale said, looking down. "His heart's not what it should be, though, and the doctors say he ought to be taking it easy."

"I know you're very concerned for him."

"The hotel remodel could bring in enough for him and Mom to live on comfortably, especially if Sudie and I pay off the mortgage early. We have the money for that, but Dad's fighting us on it. Only makes sense, though. The house and everything else will come to the two of us eventually."

Petra nodded her understanding. "You would take over the business, I presume."

Dale nodded. "Dad would still get a cut, but I think I can make it pay well enough to start thinking about a family of my own, even in these tough economic times."

Petra waited, gaze averted, for him to say more.

"I want a wife and family more than anything, and I know God has someone in store for me."

"I'm sure He does," Petra said softly.

Could it possibly be her? she wondered. She had never considered anything that even remotely resembled what Dale envisioned for himself, but she couldn't deny that he drew her as nothing else ever had. All of the Bowens did. The way they loved and enjoyed each other made her feel that she'd missed something important somewhere. But could being a part of them be enough for her?

Nell took a tumble in the gravel then. Dale sat up, Callie asleep against his shoulder.

"I'll get her," Petra said, coming to her feet.

She thought for an instant that he might refuse her assistance, but then he slumped back against the table. Petra hurried as fast as her touchy ankle would allow and crouched down beside the little girl crying in the gravel.

"Here, let me see," she said, running her hands and her gaze over the child's limbs. Nell had a red spot on one knee, but the skin wasn't even broken. "It's not too bad," Petra told her. Nell promptly reached up and wrapped her arms around Petra's neck, snuffling into her shoulder.

Petra awkwardly rose, juggling the child's weight. Nell had sense enough to wrap her legs around Petra's waist, which stabilized them both. Carefully, Petra carried the girl back to the table. By the time she arrived, Dale had belted a groggy Callie into her car seat, stowed the basket and started the engine running to cool off the van. Petra handed off Nell and got in on the passenger side.

Dale would be an amazing father, Petra thought, and an amazing husband. She just didn't know if she should even try to be the kind of partner that such a man deserved. She knew that she didn't want to be Sudie. She needed...*more*. She just didn't know if she was capable of marriage, parenthood *and* more.

When they arrived back at the hotel, only twenty or so minutes later than usual, Dale got out to open her door. Before she could exit the vehicle, however, Nell called to her.

"Pet-a! Pet-a!"

Dale shrugged when Petra looked to him in confusion, so she got out and opened the back door of the van to speak to the girl.

"Yes, Nell?"

Leaning forward, Nell puckered up her little lips for a kiss. Petra's heart turned over. She stuck her head inside the van and kissed that little pucker.

"Bye-bye," Nell said happily.

"Goodbye, sweetie."

She straightened, her heart in her throat, and nodded mutely at Dale. He brushed a finger across her cheek.

"You'll thank Hilda for us?"

"Yes," Petra answered.

His hand cupped her jaw as he softly said, "Kids are not really so mysterious, you know. Mostly it's a matter of time and attention."

That's what I'm afraid of, Petra thought, remembering all those times that she wished her parents had been there to give her the attention she needed.

Dale went around and got behind the steering wheel. Petra walked up onto the sidewalk and waved as the van pulled away from the curb. Her chest felt heavy as she watched Dale and his nieces drive away.

He made it sound so simple and easy, and for him she guessed it was. He lived right there in the house with his nieces, after all, and their mother did not divide her time between job and family. Sudie had all the time in the world to give to her girls, so any extra attention that Uncle Dale could provide must seem like icing on the cake. But what if those were his children and his wife was holding down a full-time job? How simple and easy would it be then?

Yet for the first time, Petra felt an emptiness in her life that had nothing to do with her career struggles. Why couldn't she be as close to her family as Dale was to his? And what about later in life? Now that Asher was married, he and Ellie were bound to start a family of their own one day, and Dallas fully intended to become a mother at some point. She had always said that teaching was the best of all possible careers for a woman with children because of the schedule. Maybe Phillip would even come down off his mountain long enough to meet someone. Petra wondered if she could be happy just being the aunt to the children of her siblings, as her own aunties seemed to be?

She thought of those summer visits to Chatam House and

wondered if she would be able to offer as much of herself to her nieces or nephews as Hypatia, Magnolia and Odelia had. None of them had ever worked a day for pay, after all, so they had been readily available to provide holidays for the progeny of their siblings. If she stuck to her plan, Petra suddenly realized, she wouldn't be able to offer more than a week or two of vacation time, if that. Could her determination to have a career be costing her more than it offered?

Looking down, she saw tiny smudges on her good suit jacket, but the tears that gathered in her eyes had nothing to do with smudges on her expensive jacket and everything to do with bruises on her heart.

Chapter Eleven

Her doubts stayed with Petra throughout the afternoon and church that evening, a conversation with Dexter and Garth via teleconference at the hotel the next morning, a lengthy and detailed discussion with the city office of building codes later in the day and a visit to the architect in Dallas on Friday. Meanwhile, Dale spent nearly all of his time at Chatam House putting the finishing touches on Odelia and Kent's new suite.

Petra found, to her dismay, that she missed him, having grown used to him popping in and out of her office every few hours. Talking to him on the phone about business two or three times in the same period just did not satisfy, especially as they both seemed too busy for anything personal. She knew, of course, that he went home every evening to joke and play with his nieces and the rest of the family, and she couldn't help feeling left out somehow. The sentiment did not fill her with pride. It actually frightened her.

She made up her mind to break their date on Saturday, but when she joined the aunties for breakfast that morning, they were all abuzz over her plans.

"Do you remember the time we went to the Renaissance Festival?" Hypatia asked.

Petra thought back, remembering not just the festival but also the day when Chester had come to collect her at her home in Waco. The aunties often had all the children to visit at one time, but they liked to see them one-on-one every so often, too. All of ten years old, Petra hadn't wanted to go. Being sent off alone hadn't seemed like a very good time. She'd climbed into the car so reluctantly that her mother had scolded her.

Then Maryanne had hugged her and said, "I'll miss you, but I don't want you to miss this special time with your aunties."

And it had been a special time. Hypatia had taken Petra to the Renaissance Festival, just the two of them. The other patrons had stared at Hypatia in her silk, pearls and pumps and called her "Milady." Petra had felt that she was out with the Queen of England. By the end of the day, she had wished that Hypatia was her mother rather than Maryanne. For the first time, she felt a little ashamed about that now.

"Dale will be so proud to have you on his arm," Odelia predicted, interrupting her reverie.

"Such a nice young man," Magnolia said. "Garrett quite likes him." As if that should be all anyone would ever need to know about Dale Bowen.

They liked Dale so very much and seemed so pleased that she would go out with him that Petra couldn't bear to disappoint them. Or herself. For the truth was, she very much wanted to go.

"My lady! My lady!"

Dale looked up at the "archer" on guard at the gate to the permanent, medieval-style, walled village erected among the rolling hills several miles outside of Buffalo Creek and saw that he pointed to Petra.

"Someone has stolen the crown of thy hat, my lady," the costumed man teased, referring to the canvas visor that she wore with a blousy, lightweight poet's shirt belted loosely over a pair of skinny red jeans and canvas shoes.

Laughing, Petra tossed her head, causing her ponytail to swing to and fro. "I fear you are right, good sir," she called, getting into the spirit of the thing. Dale was surprised. He hadn't expected her to get into the spirit of the thing.

"May I suggest a visit to Lady Flora's Hat Shoppe to rectify thy plight?" The archer held out his hands, palms up, in the bright sunshine. "Should it rain, thou hast no protection for thy pate!"

"My pate will survive," she said with a laugh, walking beside Dale as they followed Garrett, Jessa and their young son, Hunter, into the crowd milling about the dusty streets. "The place has grown since I was here last," she said.

"I imagine so. They add two or three new shops and attractions every year."

They caught up to the Willows family as they paused at a crossroads to study the carved wooden signs.

"What will it be first?" Garrett asked. "Belly dancing, mud wrestling, jugglers, birds of prey, bagpipers…"

"Mud wrestling!" Hunter exclaimed.

"Bagpipers," Jessa insisted. "Everyone says they're the best show here."

Garrett glanced at Dale and Petra for permission before agreeing. "Bagpipes it is, but don't think we're skipping the mud wrestlers. Or the belly dancers," he added with a waggle of his black brows.

Jessa punched him in the biceps. "Just for that, I want to see Don Juan Carletti next."

"He's the guy with the whip, right?" Dale asked.

"I'm told he's dreamy," Jessa said to Petra with a grin.

"I'm told he's an insurance agent," Garrett muttered. Petra and Jessa burst out laughing, much to Hunter's confusion. The next instant, a Viking with a horned helmet and sword caught the boy's attention, and he was gone in a flash. Garrett sped off after him, while Jessa laughed again and shook her head.

Dale bent and spoke softly into Petra's ear. "Kid was afraid of his own shadow not too long ago."

"I can understand why," she whispered. "I was at Asher's wedding when Hunter's natural father attempted to kidnap him."

"Glad they don't have to worry about that anymore," Dale muttered. Jessa's abusive ex-husband was now safely locked away in prison where he belonged.

Garrett dragged the boy back by his wrist. "You can't take off like that, buddy. It's too easy to get lost in this crowd."

"You'd find me," Hunter said confidently.

"I would," Garrett agreed, "but think of all the fun we could be having while I was looking for you."

"And think of the trouble you'd be in when I got you home," Jessa added pointedly.

Hunter hung his head. "Yes, ma'am."

She ruffled the boy's brown hair, and Garrett leaned in to kiss her cheek. Dale beamed on the Willows family, despite the way his heart squeezed in his chest. He wanted what Garrett had, and he couldn't help wondering if he was wasting his time with Petra. Even if her parents should deem a lowly carpenter fit for their daughter—and the more he knew about them, the more he doubted it—he didn't know if she could ever incorporate marriage and family into her goals. Even if she should, he wasn't sure if he could be happy with that.

His envy must have shown on his face, for as they once again fell in behind the Willows trio, she softly said, "I think you'd like to be a dad."

"Absolutely," he told her.

"Could you go for a ready-made situation like Garrett's?"

"For the right woman," he answered unhesitatingly. He ducked his head to look at her over the rim of his shades, adding, "Although, starting from scratch would be ideal."

Petra fell silent. He could almost hear her thinking about what that meant. Starting from scratch meant babies, and babies meant diapers and feedings and round-the-clock care, the kind that a mommy could best provide. Lots of women worked and had babies, of course, but Dale knew that he wouldn't want an infant of his raised by nannies or sitters. Some professional women were fortunate enough to be able to stay home for a few years, but he realized that many failed to return to the work force at all or found their careers stymied when they did. If he knew that, then Petra undoubtedly did, too.

Again, he wondered if he was wasting his time with her. Not that it mattered. He knew he'd spend every moment with her that he could. Besides, they were having great fun.

Dale had been to the Renaissance Festival so often over the years that he could recite several of the shows line for line, but he took fresh joy in seeing Hunter and Jessa experience it for the first time. Even Petra seemed agog at much that took place, oohing and aahing over the costumes and shows. She shuddered at the sword swallower and cheered during the joust. Much to Hunter's delight, she and Jessa had flowers painted on their cheeks and attached colorful veils to the backs of their visors. Armed with a newly purchased sword carved of wood, Hunter especially enjoyed a demonstration of trained dogs that herded everything from camels to ducks.

"I bet my cat, Curly, could do that," he said, while the adults traded amused looks.

By late afternoon, stuffed with turkey legs and anything the cooks could get on a stick, the boy was too tired to walk and Petra had begun to limp. With heat shimmering up off the dusty ground, Jessa pronounced it time to head home.

They prodded the boy out to the edge of the grassy parking area, but then Garrett ran ahead to get Jessa's delivery van and drive it around to pick up his wife and son. Petra insisted on walking to Dale's truck, but about halfway there he got tired of watching her limp along and swept her up in his arms to carry her. She laughed and protested, but he liked carrying her, and he knew her ankle had begun to pain her.

On the ride back to Chatam House, they chatted about the day, recounting their favorite parts.

"You have to admit," she said, "that Don Juan was very good."

"For an insurance agent," he qualified dryly. A lavishly handsome man, despite the leotard and lace, the fellow certainly could crack a whip, but Dale hadn't liked the way that he flirted with all the women in the audience, even if it was part of the act. It didn't help that Petra had seemed rapt during the performance.

She cut him a speaking look, chuckled and said, "What about that guy who sat down at the picnic table with us?"

"Sir Alonzo del Fuego *Miller,*" Dale recalled. "Did you notice that he never once dropped the sixteenth-century vernacular? We must've talked half an hour, and it was always 'thee' and 'thou' and 'at the behest of the hostler.' Pretty interesting job, training horses for the joust."

Talk went on in that vein until he pulled the truck to a stop in front of Chatam House. He got out and went around to open the door for her, but she put up a hand to stop him from helping her out.

"I'm fine."

"You're hurting," he countered, watching her gingerly climb down from the truck. She turned at the edge of the brick walkway and parked her hands at her waist.

"I spent the day at a Renaissance Festival. I think I can manage to get into the house."

He held up his hands in surrender. "It's your ankle," he said, sauntering forward. "Just remember that I can always carry you if need be."

She spluttered with laughter. "You like playing the he-man, don't you?"

"Gets you into my arms," he quipped.

She sobered then, her whole face falling into a sad frown. "I'm not sure that's wise."

"Me, either," he had to admit, though it hurt to do so.

"I—I'm just not sure that we want the same things," she said, making it sound as much a question as a statement.

Dale sighed. "I know."

"Doesn't seem much point to it then, does there?" she asked softly.

"I guess not."

Now that they'd both voiced their doubts, he supposed that was that. Oh, how he wished he'd kept his clever quip behind his teeth! But what good would that do?

After a moment, she said, "Thank you. I had a great time."

"Me, too," he told her. The urge to kiss her again seized him, so he hastily stepped back. "See you tomorrow. At work."

She nodded, and he turned away, coiling his hands into fists as he hurried around to the driver's seat of the truck.

What was it Corinthians said? He recalled the verse as he drove away from her.

"No temptation has overtaken you except what is common to mankind. And God is faithful; He will not let you be tempted beyond what you can bear. But when you are tempted, He will also provide a way out so that you can endure it."

"Well, I'm enduring it, Lord," he said aloud, "but I don't see a way out." Not the one he wanted to see, anyway.

Waving at Sudie Baker across the wide sanctuary, Petra put a smile on her face, but Hypatia noted that it did not reach her eyes. Glancing back, she saw that Dale Bowen was studiously avoiding so much as a peek in Petra's direction.

Oh, dear. Trouble. And Hypatia had thought the two young people were getting on so well.

Petra sank down on the pew and looked straight ahead, but her stoicism did not fool Hypatia.

"Is something wrong, dear?" she asked softly.

Petra shook her head, her gaze dropping to her lap.

"Didn't you and Dale have a good time yesterday?" Hypatia asked cautiously.

"Oh, yes," Petra said, but the eyes that she so briefly turned Hypatia's way shone suspiciously bright.

Hypatia wrapped an arm around her niece. Few had ever understood the fierce intelligence or sensitive nature of this child. Petra alone among her brother Murdock's children had doubted herself, setting such impossibly high standards that she was bound to fail. It was not enough for Petra to excel; she had to be the best at whatever she tried. She was much more like her mother, Maryanne, than anyone realized. If only she would believe in herself, she could do anything. She could do things that Hypatia herself could not, like the woman worth far more than rubies. That reminded Hypatia of her advice to her niece when last they'd spoken privately together.

"Dear, have you had a chance to look over that chapter in Proverbs yet?"

"Oh, no. I'm sorry. I haven't. Which one was it?"

"The thirty-first. If you're pressed for time, you can start at verse ten. I think it might clarify a thing or two for you."

"I'll read it, I promise," Petra said with a wan smile.

Hypatia hugged her and made a mental promise to spend some concentrated time in prayer on Petra's behalf. She had been remiss in her prayers, with Odelia's wedding just days away, but that would change, starting now.

What a long, dismal day, Petra thought, walking into her room at Chatam House. For the first time in her memory, church had not soothed her. Just knowing that Dale was in the building and that he would not be seeking her out had nearly brought her to tears, but what other choice did they have? He wanted a wife like his mother and sister. Petra couldn't imagine not working at something, but she didn't want to be like her own mother, too often called away when her children needed her.

Still, never to have a child of her own! Petra had discounted children long ago. She had considered marriage and motherhood the price she would have to pay to at last fit in with her family. But what of her family? Her parents were still consumed by their individual medical practices. Asher had his career and now a wife. They would undoubtedly start a family before long. Phillip was off on a mountain somewhere, and Dallas…at least her meddling kept her involved in Petra's life, but Dallas had made no secret of the fact that she expected to marry as soon as she'd found her "Mr. Perfect."

Then how will I fit? Petra wondered morosely, but she had no answer for that dilemma. Tired as she was, she feared she might be in for a long, sleepless night.

While changing into her nightclothes and taking down her hair, she thought about Hypatia's gentle insistence that she read Proverbs. She told herself that she might as well. She didn't have anything else to do, after all. Settling on the sofa in the sitting area with her Bible in hand, she thumbed through it to the thirty-first chapter of Proverbs and began to read. When she came to the tenth verse, she sat up straight and concentrated, reading aloud.

"A wife of noble character who can find? She is worth far more than rubies."

Petra went on reading about how such a woman's husband would have full confidence in her and how busy she would be providing for her family and servants. Why, she would even venture into businesses, buying fields and planting vineyards, trading profitably.

"'Her children arise and call her blessed,'" Petra read, "'her husband also, and he praises her: 'Many women do noble things, but you surpass them all.' Charm is deceptive, and beauty is fleeting; but a woman who fears the LORD is to be praised. Honor her for all that her hands have done, and let her works bring her praise at the city gate.'"

Petra let the Bible fall to her lap. That didn't sound like a housebound woman to her. That almost sounded like a business woman! In fact, it almost sounded like her mother!

Of course, nothing said that a housewife couldn't be as industrious as the woman of Proverbs, and Petra felt sure that most were, especially those with children. And yet…nothing here said that a woman could not, should not, work outside her home, either, only that her home and family should be the central purpose of her labor. The decision to work outside her home, Petra supposed, God left up to every couple to make for themselves. Each situation was surely different, and so it was up to each married couple to prayerfully choose the best path for them and their family.

She began to read the passage again, pausing when she came to the part that mentioned servants. Well, that didn't apply to this modern era. Unless…might not nannies and housekeepers, even part-time babysitters, apply here? They certainly deserved their portion like everyone else.

Petra thought of how her mother had always appreciated the staff and chosen them so carefully. Petra had resented them, though, because they were not Maryanne. How many times in her mother's absence had one of them reminded her of the important work that her mother did? Petra realized suddenly that she didn't want to do work that might be more important than her family, not even on minor occasions.

Suddenly thankful that she had not been called to medicine or some other equally demanding career, Petra tried to picture her future in light of the revelation in this passage. There was room in God's plan for marriage and career, for housewives who labored in the home and career women who labored outside of it. So long as home and family were at the heart of a woman's labors, it mattered not *where* she labored or at what.

Petra felt as if a great weight had been lifted from her shoulders. This really was not an either/or situation. She didn't have to go into acquisitions at Anderton Hotels. It wasn't necessary to go to Europe. She could balance a job and a husband and children. If she could manage that, she would be a success. She would be a "woman worth more than rubies!"

Of course, she should always put the welfare of her family first, and whatever work she chose didn't have to make anybody's list of "best occupations." It didn't have to win awards or make world-changing contributions to society. She had not been called to that. Whatever she did, though, it had to give her a sense of accomplishment and personal achievement. Much like what she was doing now.

She enjoyed the work she was currently doing, but she had enjoyed many, even most, of her jobs. Dale had told her that she was a good manager. Maybe she would enjoy managing the hotel as much as she enjoyed overseeing the renovation of it. She could do that job and be married, too. She thought of Jessa Willows and how she worked side by side with her husband. Petra had told herself that theirs was a unique situation, and so it was, but if Garrett had stayed at Chatam House as the gardener, surely they'd have found a way to make it all work. Now, if only Dale could see things that way!

But he didn't. At least, she didn't think he did.

They hadn't really discussed it.

Still, all things considered, she felt that she could safely assume that he wanted a stay-at-home wife like his mom and sister.

That meant that she was really no better off now than before. However much she might want to be what he wanted, she just didn't think that could be her.

Deflated once again, she put aside her Bible and went to bed, but sleep, as she had feared, was long in coming, despite the prayers she whispered late into the night.

Chapter Twelve

"I just don't understand what you're doing," Dallas said, sitting down in one of a pair of mismatched chairs in front of Petra's desk on Monday morning.

Adopting a brisk tone, Petra stated the obvious. "I was working. Now I'm talking to you."

"I'm talking about Dale Bowen," Dallas exclaimed bluntly. "You're dating him!"

Was dating him, Petra silently amended, taken off guard by the lance of pain in her chest. She said, "It doesn't mean anything."

"Well, I should hope not," Dallas retorted. "I mean, I'm sure he's a very nice man, and he's attractive enough—"

"Attractive enough?" Petra repeated, shocked. He was more than attractive, for pity's sake. He was breathtaking, inhumanly handsome. The sight of him, the *thought* of him, made Petra's heart pound, and Dallas called him "handsome enough"?

"And he's a real stand-up kind of guy, too," Dallas plunged on, "according to Garrett. But you have to admit that he's just not in the same league as Garth Anderton."

That much was true. Garth and Dale were as different as two men could be. Garth was urbane, professionally groomed, wealthy, driven. Dale was salt-of-the-earth, handsome without even trying, moderately successful, laid-back, loving—and apparently not interested enough in her to adjust his requirements of a wife. Or was he?

She had assumed, obviously, that they wanted different things out of life, but that didn't seem quite so obvious anymore. Petra now knew that she didn't have to be happy with just a career anymore than she had to be happy with just a marriage. Could Dale be happy with a working wife, though?

Oh, if only he'd argued with her when she'd said there was no point in them seeing each other! But he hadn't. He had, in fact, agreed with her.

Maybe Dallas was right. Maybe she was pining after the wrong man.

Whenever Petra tried to picture herself with Garth, however, the best she could do involved a business suit, a briefcase and a clipboard. When she pictured herself with Dale, they were sitting side by side on a couch or a park bench, laughing and talking. Or he was holding her in his arms, toting her around like a favorite toy, smiling down at her with those rich green eyes, as if she could be the center of his personal universe.

She shivered, missing him with a sharp, aching pang. It didn't matter that his world felt so foreign to her. Even her confusion and misgivings seemed unimportant compared to this feeling that she had when she thought of him.

She shook her head, muttering, "None of that matters."

"Listen," Dallas said, pecking a fingertip on the desktop. "I get it. I really do. The aunties are thrilled. They couldn't wait to tell me about your dates with Dale Bowen. But don't you see? They'd be thrilled if it was Garth, too, and he's so much better suited to you."

Narrowing her eyes, Petra asked, "What makes you think he and I would suit?"

Dallas spread her hands. "Well, it's obvious! He's just so…

like you, so effective and good-looking and polished. Not to mention expensive. I mean, the man oozes success."

Petra frowned. Dallas made her sound like the latest model of stainless-steel refrigerator. Useful, attractive, cold. Was that how Dale saw her? Pretty, desirable, but not worth the price? Maybe he just didn't understand what the price included. In fact, he couldn't possibly because she had just figured it out herself. Might it be that he just needed a little time to get to know the new her? She bit her lip, wondering if she dared ask him out now. Suddenly inspired, she got to her feet.

"Where are you going?" Dallas squawked.

"Out," Petra answered succinctly, taking her handbag from the drawer of her desk.

"I thought you had to work!"

"Life isn't all work, Dallas," Petra lectured, enjoying the way her sister's mouth dropped open.

"Yours has been!" Dallas shot back.

"Then it's time for some changes," Petra said, as much to herself as to her sister.

Dale could not have been more surprised when Petra appeared in the suite that morning if she'd arrived in a puff of smoke.

"Hello," she said.

"Hey."

Seeming unsure of herself, she licked her lips and unconsciously widened her stance, straining the seams of the straight, navy blue skirt that she wore with a matching short-sleeved sweater. She'd left her hair down but had pulled the front back to make a little pouf on top. It was a very sophisticated look, but then she was a sophisticated woman.

Setting aside the paintbrush he'd been cleaning, Dale wiped his hands on a blue rag and gave her his full attention.

"What's up? Problem at the hotel?"

She shook her head. "No. This is personal."

Personal. Doubly surprised, he stuffed the rag into a pocket on his coveralls and spread his hands, waiting for her to speak. After what she'd said on Saturday, he couldn't imagine what personal matter she could have to discuss with him, but considering how he felt about her, he'd be a fool not to listen. Still, he braced himself. Maybe she thought she hadn't made her disinterest clear enough.

After sucking in a deep breath, she doggedly said, "I've met your parents, but you haven't met mine. I was wondering how you'd feel about having breakfast with them on Wednesday morning? They plan to leave for home again before lunch the day after the wedding."

That didn't quite compute for Dale. He tilted his head, going over her words in his mind. "Are you asking me to have breakfast with *you* and your parents?"

"On Wednesday morning," she confirmed.

She could've knocked him over with a feather. After Saturday, he hadn't expected to see her again except at work. Now here she was, asking to introduce him to her parents? That could only mean that she wasn't any more ready to give up on him than he was on her. A giddy feeling welled up inside of him, momentarily robbing him of speech. Eventually, however, he found his voice.

"Okay. Sure. But can I ask why?"

"I want you all to meet," she replied calmly. "I realized, you see, how much I learned about you by meeting your family, and I thought that meeting my parents might help you understand me."

He blinked at that. "I thought you said we were wasting our time."

"I did," she admitted, "but I'm wondering if I was wrong. I mean, we work so well together, and you must know that I…" She shook her head. "I'm not sure how I feel really, but I know I've never felt this way before."

That was good enough for him. For now. The only problem was that Wednesday suddenly seemed far, far away.

"How about dinner tonight?" he asked impulsively. "We can talk."

She made a disappointed face. "I've been invited to the rehearsal dinner tonight. I only helped write place cards for the wedding reception, but Kent insisted."

"I see. I guess you're busy tomorrow, too?" Dale pressed hopefully.

She huffed a sigh. "It's Odelia's wedding day, and frankly I don't even know what I'll be wearing yet."

"Whatever it is, you'll look beautiful," he assured her.

She smiled brightly enough to temporarily blind him. "Thank you."

"You're welcome. Uh, about Wednesday, when and where?"

"I'll have to let you know," she told him apologetically.

"That's fine."

They stood there staring stupidly at each other for several seconds before she said, "Well, I'd better get back to work."

He nodded. "Me, too. All of my gear needs to be out of here by tonight. They've already started moving in some stuff as it is. Best get to it."

Nodding, she turned to go then paused. "Will you be at the wedding?"

He had meant to attend the wedding, but after Petra had more or less broken things off with him, he'd toyed with the idea of backing out. Why torture himself by spending the evening in the same room with her? Now wild horses couldn't keep him away, even if all he could do was wave at her from a distance.

"I'll be there," he told her. "I know you'll have family around you, but maybe we'll see each other then."

She nodded. "I'll look for you."

"Do that," he encouraged, wondering if it was too late to

have his one and only suit dry cleaned. Then again, maybe he ought to buy a new one. He suddenly wanted to look his very best.

Watching Petra literally waltz across the landing from the doorway of Odelia and Kent's new suite, Hypatia smiled to herself. She turned her gaze heavenward. Well, well. Looked like her prayers had wrought a change for the better. Hypatia felt a keen sense of satisfaction at the notion of Petra and Dale together. She knew that Dallas hoped for a union between Petra and Garth Anderton, but Hypatia couldn't help feeling that Dale would be a better partner for Petra. She had nothing against Anderton. He was a charming rascal, after all, but Dale was so grounded and solid. He would prove a more than adequate partner for a professional woman, or any woman for that matter.

Slipping into the sitting room that she shared with her sisters, Hypatia found the thick portfolio that she used to organize wedding details—as much as it was possible to organize with Odelia changing her mind about something every other minute—and carried it back out onto the landing. She walked to the open doorway through which Petra had emerged and looked inside, just to be sure that she had her facts straight. Dale was packing away a paintbrush. Glancing up, he smiled at her.

"Can I help you with something?"

"No, no," she answered. "Just thought I'd look in on you."

"Ah." He glanced around. "Almost through here. I'll be out of your way before lunch."

"You've done an admirable job," Hypatia told him, "and I know Odelia and Kent appreciate it."

"It's been my pleasure," he returned, smiling.

Hypatia inclined her head. "I won't keep you any longer."

"Have a nice day."

"You, too," she replied softly, taking her leave.

For once, she decided, she was going to give the couple a bit of a nudge. Oh, it wasn't matchmaking. Not really. She had strict rules about matchmaking. She'd just give them a helpful nudge and leave the rest up to God.

She carried the portfolio downstairs to the library, where Odelia, Kent and Magnolia waited to go over last-minute details. To her surprise, Hypatia found her niece Dallas also in attendance. Apparently, she had come to admire her handiwork, as she sat smiling at Odelia and Kent, who whispered and cooed together at one end of the long table there. Magnolia rolled her eyes as Hypatia made her way to a chair.

"Before we begin, may I make a personal request?" Hypatia asked.

Kent chuckled. "Who do *you* want us to invite to the wedding?"

Hypatia frowned. "What makes you think I want you to invite someone to the wedding?"

Dallas tucked something into her small handbag and rose. "I'll be running along now."

"Must you?" Odelia asked, sounding disappointed.

"People to see, things to do," Dallas replied airily, moving toward the door. "Have a good one, gang. Ta-ta!" She went out of the room, leaving Hypatia feeling that all was not quite right.

She turned back to the table just as Odelia sighed and laid her head on Kent's shoulder. "Can you believe it? We're getting married tomorrow!"

"At long last," Kent said. Then he leaned forward and addressed Hypatia. "You were saying, dear lady?"

Shaking her head, Hypatia returned to the issue at hand. "I'd like to make a slight change in seating arrangements for the reception."

Kent and Odelia exchanged complacent looks. "Whatever you'd like, dear," Odelia chirped.

As if! Hypatia thought, but she merely smiled. "I'll take care of it later then."

Even as she pulled her checklist from the portfolio, her lips curled in a satisfied smile. Despite all that remained to be done before the wedding, she thought she could manage to alter one little seating chart.

The morning turned out to be a productive one for Petra. Even with her head in the clouds and so many uncertainties on the horizon, she felt more settled than she had in weeks. In reality, nothing had been settled. Nothing at all! Except that she knew she would continue to see Dale Bowen at every opportunity. She didn't have to wait long. He showed up with lunch at half past twelve.

"What's this?" she asked as he dropped the fast-food bag onto her desk.

"You said no to dinner, not lunch."

She laughed. "I was going to work through, make up for the personal time I took this morning."

"That's about what I figured," he told her, pulling a chair to the end of her desk while she took the burgers from the bag. "A very conscientious worker, our Petra."

"Wouldn't you want a worker in your employ to be as conscientious?" she asked.

"Yep," he admitted, "so I propose we discuss business, make it a working lunch."

She smiled. "Okay. What business did you have in mind?"

Dale peeled back the paper on his burger. "The spa presentation to the BCHS."

They discussed her ideas on that. He gave her several suggestions and tips concerning the likes and dislikes of the executive committee members. Then he casually asked, "Have you ever worked for a construction company?"

"Once," she said. "That's part of the reason Garth picked me for this job."

"I see. Thought that might be the case. You do seem to understand the terms and processes."

Petra shrugged. "I suppose. Why do you ask?"

"Thinking of doing some reorganization in the management of Bowen & Bowen," he said. "Thought I might pick your brain about that."

The idea made perfect sense to Petra. With his father stepping back in the near future, Dale would have his hands full, so a reorganization was needed.

"You're a hands-on kind of guy," she noted carefully. He nodded in agreement. "Seems to me you'll want to hire a full-time manager then, someone to schedule jobs, pay the bills and the help, negotiate contracts with suppliers. That will leave you free to handle the actual construction end of things."

"Just what I was thinking," Dale said, finishing off his burger.

They ate in silence for several seconds before Petra asked, "Do you have anyone in mind?"

"I do," he told her with a small smile. "I surely do."

"Well, that's good," she said, watching him dredge a handful of fries in ketchup and carry them to his mouth. "It always helps if you can reorganize with someone specific in mind."

"Seems like I've always got someone in mind these days," he commented softly, his gaze focusing on her.

Her heartbeat sped up just a bit. She hoped that he meant her, of course, and that eventually he'd have more in mind for her than business luncheons.

Somehow, Petra managed to get through her daily list before she had to leave the hotel. She worked hard at it after Dale's surprise luncheon, as she didn't intend to be in the office the next day. Knowing that her parents and brother Phillip would be arriving from out of town, she'd arranged ahead of time to take off the entire day Tuesday, the day of Odelia's wedding.

Petra found herself actually looking forward to the wedding. She'd dreaded it before, but Odelia's joy in every little detail of the day, coupled with her obvious love for Kent, promised to make this a very special event, perhaps because Petra wasn't afraid to enjoy a romantic moment herself now. She could even admit that a part of her had always yearned for romance, a part that she had tried very hard to bury beneath her need to succeed.

At quitting time, Petra jumped up and rushed out of the building, knowing that she only had minutes in which to get home and change. She saw an unfamiliar car pull up to the curb as she hurriedly moved down the sidewalk, but she didn't expect Garth to hop out and stride toward her.

"What are you doing here?" she asked.

"This is my hotel," he pointed out with a wry smile.

"I know that. I just meant, why aren't you in Colorado?"

"Colorado can take care of itself for a while. I'm glad I caught you, though. I wanted to suggest that we go to the wedding together tomorrow."

"The wedding?" Petra echoed, surprised. "I wasn't aware that you'd received an invitation."

He reached into the pocket of his suit coat and brought out a familiar-looking ivory envelope. "I've got it right here."

Now that was odd. Odelia and Kent had wrangled with Hypatia over every name on the guest list. Hypatia had even remarked that if she left it to them, they'd invite the whole town. No doubt, they'd decided to invite Garth in deference to the fact that he was her boss. She wished she'd known. She'd have advised against it.

"I'm sorry," she told him gently, "but my brother Phillip will be escorting me. We so seldom get to see each other, you know." It was entirely true. The two of them had jokingly arranged to be each other's escort for this wedding last month at Asher's, since it had seemed that everyone was pairing off but them.

To her relief, Garth accepted this graciously. "Very well. I'll just see you there, then."

"Of course."

Petra made the drive back to Chatam House for the second time that day and changed into a flowing pantsuit of turquoise silk before hurrying to the new suite, but when she looked in, the sitting room was empty. She turned around again, and Hypatia stood there, her handbag dangling from her wrist.

"He just carried down the last load," she said with a small, knowing smile.

Petra didn't pretend that she was not looking for Dale. Instead, she ran to catch him. She found him loading tools into the back of his truck.

"Wow. Look at you," he said, doing just that.

She laughed and quipped, "What? This old thing."

"You look like a million bucks," he told her softly. "Then again, your parents being doctors, I suppose you had a pretty privileged upbringing."

"Not really," she hastened to assure him. "Mom and Dad were quite strict about money and…" She realized that he was looking at the house behind her. She hadn't grown up in a mansion, but her parents' house was large and lavish. She suddenly didn't want him to know that, though. She didn't want him ever to think that he might not be good enough or rich enough for her, but she didn't know how to tell him that without sounding as if she hoped for more from him than she had a right to expect. "I'll tell you something," she began carefully. "I'd trade all the privilege of my upbringing for a family as close as yours."

He traced the curve of her jaw with his fingertips. "That's good to know." He dropped his hand then. "But it's not too late. I mean, maybe a closer relationship with your folks begins with you. Maybe all you have to do is reach out. Maybe they're waiting for you to make the first move. Did you ever think of that?"

She honestly hadn't. All these years, had she been waiting for everyone else to reach out to her? Had that made her seem standoffish and cool? She felt a spurt of shame that such might have been the case, but now was not the time to discuss it.

"I have to run," she said regretfully. "The others will be waiting for me. I just wanted to say good night."

"See you tomorrow," he told her, tapping her chin. She laughed because he seemed to like her version of the Chatam cleft.

"At the wedding," she confirmed. "And Wednesday for breakfast."

"And Wednesday for breakfast. Just let me know where and when."

She nodded, smiling, and he got into the truck. After starting the engine, he lifted a hand in farewell then backed the truck around the corner of the house. She followed on foot, watching until the white pickup turned onto the street, then she joined her aunts and Kent in the town car.

No one was surprised when Petra's parents called to say they couldn't make the rehearsal. Petra stood in for her absent father, dutifully walking Odelia down the aisle. The rest of the time, she was able to sit quietly and think about what Dale had said to her. She concluded that she had been somewhat petulant in her attitude toward her immediate family. Apparently, that disgruntled little girl had not quite grown up, and it was past time for that to happen. She promised herself that she would no longer sulk about the lack of attention that she'd received from her parents and siblings. She would, instead, begin to pay attention to them.

Given the lighthearted mood, the rehearsal dinner turned into a jovial affair. Nevertheless, the aunties wanted to make an early night of it, so they returned to the house around eight-thirty to find that Phillip had arrived from Seattle. He stood in the entry hall surrounded by a trio of bags. Before the aunties could even get over their surprise, Petra went to hug him. Her tall, lanky brother, who had dark, wavy hair to go with his copper-brown eyes, seemed almost taken aback.

"What? I'm not allowed to miss my brother?" she teased, adding playfully, "Don't forget you're my escort to the wedding."

"As if you need my escort," he said.

"Oh, no," Petra ribbed, shaking a finger at him, "you're not getting out of it that easily. We had a deal."

"Very well," Phillip agreed, smiling. "You're in a happy mood."

Dallas wandered out of the parlor just then, their parents in tow.

Once again surprised, Petra turned her attention to Maryanne and Murdock. She noted the anxious look in her mother's eyes, and for the first time considered that it might have less to do with her perceived "failures" than her attitude.

"Mother," she said, then immediately amended the greeting to, "Mom. I didn't expect you and Dad this evening."

"I know we missed the rehearsal," Maryanne told her, "but we decided to come tonight anyway."

It was typical Maryanne and Murdock to show up late, but Petra supposed it was characteristic of most doctors. She determined to put aside her resentment and just enjoy the company of her parents for a change. Walking forward with outstretched arms, she said, "I'm glad. Gives us more time to visit."

She caught the look of surprise on her father's patrician face as she enveloped her mother in a hug.

That's one more to Dale Bowen's credit, Petra thought.

Thank You, Lord, for bringing such a wise man into my life!

Chapter Thirteen

When Petra entered the vestibule of the chapel at Downtown Bible Church the next evening with her parents, she immediately saw her brother Asher, looking handsome and distinguished in his tuxedo. He chuckled at something her sister-in-law Ellie said and wrapped his arms around her. Ash had always seemed older than his years, Petra mused, and it was only partly because of that prematurely graying hair of his—if graying was the right word for the distinguished slashes of champagne-pale hair at his chestnut temples. He had always seemed to carry the weight of the world on his athletic shoulders, but now he looked so relaxed and happy. Ellie tipped her head back, smiling, and Ash kissed her, long and sweetly.

Oh, how she wanted that, Petra mused, more than she'd ever imagined! She supposed that she'd always wanted it in the secret recesses of her heart, but only since meeting Dale Bowen had she realized it. Was that a sign of God's will for her life? Had God picked out Dale for her? She hoped so. All this time, she'd eschewed romance and assumed that she should concentrate on her career. No wonder she hadn't found her calling yet. She'd been looking in all the wrong places.

Her parents traded looks beside her, silently watching their son and daughter-in-law embrace. Petra noticed that her father's hand came up to rest possessively in the small of her mother's back. They were not demonstrative people, but Petra saw in that one small gesture a fondness that she had always sensed yet rarely witnessed between her parents. She saw, too, the quiet pleasure they took in Asher's happiness. Maybe the Chatams would never tease with the ease of the Bowens, and they would certainly never live together in one house again, but they loved each other and they could share that love openly—with a little encouragement.

So caught up in each other were the young couple that they only broke apart when Murdock cleared his throat.

"Ah," Asher said, spinning about, "there you are. Glad you're early. Aunt Odelia is worried you won't know how to give away the bride."

"I'd better go to her," Murdock announced. "I'll see you all later."

Ellie offered to show him where to find his sister, and they went off together. The door opened again just then. Asher turned, ready to do his duty as an usher, only to relax as Phillip joined them, then looked around and asked, "Where's Dad?"

"Where do you think?" Petra returned. "With the bride, of course."

"Of course. What about Dallas?"

"Right here," came the answer. She must have caught the door before it closed behind Phillip. "And look who I found on the sidewalk outside."

Petra turned to find Garth smiling at her. He looked stunningly handsome in a suit that probably cost more than Odelia's bridal gown, and Petra wished mightily that he had come just a little later, especially when he so determinedly set out to charm her mother and brothers. He had met everyone but Phillip in the months that she'd worked for him, and they seemed to like him well enough, Dallas especially. Petra had reason to wish him all the way back to Colorado a few minutes later when he somehow managed to maneuver it so he, instead of Phillip, wound up sitting next to her in the pew near the front of the chapel. Dallas played a part in that, too, and Petra determined to speak to her sister later in private about her tendency to meddle.

The only man who interested Petra was Dale Bowen, and she would proudly admit it.

Don laughed when Dale came downstairs in a new dark blue suit and tie.

"Well, I think you look very nice," Sudie told him, straightening the knot in his blue-and-green patterned tie, which he wore with a snow-white shirt.

"Thanks, sis," he said, breathing a tiny sigh of relief. He couldn't help remembering Garth Anderton's expensive tailored suits and hand-sewn shirts, though. Even the best that Buffalo Creek had to offer wouldn't equal a cuff link at Anderton's wrist, but Dale had done the best he could.

"Say hello to Petra for us," his mother called as he hurried from the house with the heavy package that she had wrapped for him, antique fire tools for the fireplace in Odelia and Kent's suite.

He drove his mom's sedan to the church. Petra's brother, Attorney Asher Chatam, greeted Dale with a handshake at the chapel door.

"Bride's side or groom's?" Asher asked, smiling.

"I imagine your sister is sitting on the bride's side," Dale mused aloud.

The tuxedoed attorney's eyebrows arched at the same time that his lips curled up. "Of course. Both of them."

"I don't suppose you could find me a seat near Petra?" Dale asked.

Asher grinned and handed him a pink program. "I think that can be arranged. Follow me."

Dale smiled when he saw that Petra sat on the end of a pew near the front of the church. She had put up her pale gold hair in a sleek, sophisticated roll against the back of her neck. All Dale could see of her hot pink dress was the back of the high, round neck and sleeveless bodice. A triangular cutout exposed the delicate curves of her shoulder blades. He wondered if she was too cool in the chilled room and imagined wrapping his arms around her. Waving off Asher's assistance, he quietly walked up and laid a hand on her shoulder. She glanced up and smiled before making room for him to squeeze in next to her. That's when he realized that Garth Anderton sat on her other side.

Anderton glared daggers at him, but before anyone could speak, the pianist began to play. Dale looked to the grand piano at the front of the slightly sloping chapel and saw that a young blonde woman in an understated pink gown sat at the instrument, plying it with serious concentration and even greater skill. The music seemed to literally flow from her fingertips. He checked his program, but before he found a name to assign to the musician, Petra leaned her head close to his ear and whispered, "My cousin Lyric. She and her sister, Harmony, will both play."

"Ah."

Knowing that his mother and sister would want details, Dale took note of the decorations, a profusion of creamy white camellias and pale pink roses, satin ribbon and glimmering netting. He had to admit that the effect was quite pretty, from the huge arrangements placed atop short, Grecian-style columns scattered around the platform at the front of the sanctuary to those gracing the ends of the pews. Dozens of tiny votive candles flickered from the top of the rectangular altar, leaving just enough space for a simple gold cross in the center.

A door at one side of the front of the church opened, and Hubner Chatam, the elder brother of the triplets and the retired former pastor of the church, walked out in clerical robes, followed by the groom and Magnolia Chatam, attired in what could only be described as a skirted tuxedo. She'd wrapped her head in a coronet of braids into which a spray of pink rosebuds had been tucked. Kent wore a traditional black tuxedo with a pink-and-white-striped vest over a white shirt and pink bow tie.

Hub took his place before the altar. Both Kent and Magnolia turned to face the back of the church. The doors at the rear of the sanctuary opened. Asher and Reeves Leland, another Chatam nephew, unrolled a white satin aisle cloth before taking seats beside their respective wives.

Next came Hunter, Garrett's stepson, and pretty little curly-top Gilli Latimer, Reeve's daughter, all decked out in frothy pink, her skirts bouncing as she strewed pink rose petals from the basket that Hunter carried. When the small pair reached the altar, Hunter simply upended the basket and dumped the remaining petals in a heap on the gold carpet. Kent chuckled as the children darted off to sit with their parents. Dallas groaned audibly, and Garth shook his head, but Dale exchanged an amused glance with Petra as Magnolia quickly spread the petals with her foot. He found the unrehearsed moments the most fun part of any wedding ceremony, and Petra seemed to share his sentiment.

Heads turned toward the central aisle again as Hypatia Chatam appeared and began a slow, graceful stroll to the front of the church. Wearing a suit of pale pink satin with a long skirt and a jacket scattered with pearls, she had twisted her silver hair into its usual neat chignon and adorned it with a pearl encrusted comb. In her hands, she carried a small, round bouquet of pink roses and camellias. As Hypatia took her place at the front of the church, the music faded away.

Utter silence followed while a second young woman

joined the first on the piano bench. Hot pink streaked her pale blond, chin-length hair, and she wore a pink and yellow chiffon dress with fingerless net gloves.

"Twins," Petra whispered pointedly. "Identical," she added.

Dale lifted his eyebrows. "Not when it comes to personal taste," he muttered from the corner of his mouth, frowning when Garth shushed him. Petra bit her lips against a knowing smile and lightly bumped her shoulder against him as if to say he should pay Garth no mind. Mollified, Dale fixed his attention on the piano.

Harmony's unconventional costume did not prevent her from playing the piano every bit as well as her sister. Dale recognized a complicated version of an old hymn, "Just As I Am," an unusual choice for a wedding, to be sure.

At the start of the chorus, Kent broke into a wide smile, and the gathering rose as one to turn toward the aisle. Odelia Chatam stood in the open doorway on the arm of a tall, slender, dignified man of middle age. His thick, yellow-white hair had been brushed straight back from his high forehead, and he wore his tuxedo with an ivory white cummerbund and tie that perfectly matched Odelia's dress. Dale barely noticed. He was stunned by Odelia Chatam.

He'd seen Odelia in some outrageous getups, but this... this was downright glamorous.

Her white hair had been curled into a froth held back from her face by an ivory satin headband to which an organza camellia, set with rhinestones, had been affixed, just above her right ear. Sparkling silver chains hung from her earlobes, anchored on each end by sizable diamonds. Around her throat, she wore a strand of pearls with a heart-shaped diamond clasp. The fitted satin bodice featured a high, square neckline and a lace overlay that turned into long sleeves, which flared elegantly at the wrists. A column of lace tiers comprised the long skirt. Across her body draped a wide satin sash, beauty-queen style, attached at the left shoulder with a satin flower at least six inches wide. In her hands, she carried a teardrop-shaped bouquet of camellias.

Odelia may have waited fifty years to be a bride, but no bride of any age had ever looked more radiant. Dale had rarely seen the woman when she wasn't smiling, but today she literally glowed. As she strolled down the aisle, Kent puffed up with such pride that Dale began to fear he would lift off like a helium balloon.

"Someone should tie an anchor to the groom," he muttered to Petra, smiling.

When she failed to reply, he glanced at her, and was shocked to see tears rolling from her eyes. Dallas reached past Garth to offer Petra a tissue. She took it with one hand and slipped the other through the crook of Dale's elbow, following Odelia with her gaze. Catching a movement from the corner of his eye, Dale half turned to find that Garth had lifted a comforting hand to Petra's shoulder. She tossed Anderton a tight smile and dropped her hand from Dale's arm. Dale resisted the urge to proclaim that Petra was his and pop Anderton on the end of his nose with a fist.

Hub Chatam gave the guests leave to sit. As soon as they did so, he intoned, "We are gathered here to join in holy wedlock Kent Hollister Monroe and Odelia Mae Chatam. Who gives the bride in marriage?"

Her escort answered, "Her brothers and sisters." Then he placed Odelia's hand in Kent's and stepped back to take a seat beside a woman who looked remarkably like Petra, despite the gray streaking her shoulder-length blond hair.

Kaylie Chatam Gallow, Petra's cousin, rose and moved to a small lectern near the piano. Opening a book on the lectern, she began to read in a clear, lilting voice, Shakespeare's twenty-second sonnet. "'My glass shall not persuade me I am old. So long as youth and thou are of one date…'"

Petra dabbed at her cheeks with the tissue, looking so achingly beautiful that Dale couldn't take his eyes off her long enough to concentrate on the verse. When Kaylie finished, Bayard, Kaylie's brother, got up and moved to the lectern. He had often sung at Downtown Bible Church when his father, Hub, had been pastor here, but it had been years since Dale had last heard him. He did not disappoint, singing in a towering tenor that mesmerized everyone.

When the song ended, Odelia sniffed, and Kent, true to form, instantly whipped out a handkerchief the size of a tablecloth. She giggled, which produced a ripple of laughter among the guests. Even Hypatia chuckled. Petra laughed aloud, and that made Dale smile and squeeze her hand.

Morgan, another of Kaylie's brothers, got up and read a long selection from the Book of Ruth. Then Hubner once again took center stage, asking the traditional questions and receiving the traditional replies of "I do." Then he announced that the couple had prepared their own vows. Dale felt the crowd draw a collective breath as they waited to hear what these two would say. Odelia passed her bouquet to Hypatia and gave her hands to Kent, who spoke first.

"My darling," he said in a voice gravelly with emotion, "fifty years is not too long to wait for you. I would wait another fifty if I must, but I am so very grateful that I won't have to! Before God and these witnesses, I promise to be a faithful, true and considerate husband and to shower you with all the love the human heart can hold. In sickness and in health, poverty or wealth, joy or sorrow, I will never willingly leave your side 'til death do us part. I give you my solemn vow."

Magnolia produced a ring, which he then slid onto Odelia's finger. She made a noise about it, sighing, "So beautiful!" Then it was her turn.

"I have loved but one man in my life with the love that a wife might feel for her husband," she said, gazing into his eyes. "It has always been you. I will always love you so, and before God and these witnesses, I promise to be ever at your side, faithful and true, no matter what comes, 'til death do us part. I give you my solemn vow."

Petra gave a little laughing sob as Odelia removed a ring from her thumb and fit it onto Kent's finger, with some effort and several giggles. Dale reached over and laid a hand over her wrist, receiving a tremulous smile in return. Had she envisioned, as he had, the two of them standing there? She glanced away, and he realized Garth had taken her hand on the other side. Dale pulled back, doing his best to tamp down his temper as Hub spoke a short but eloquent prayer before lifting his gaze on the couple standing before him.

"And now," he said, raising his right hand, "as you have consented before our Heavenly Father and these witnesses to love, honor and cherish one another, I pronounce you husband and wife. Go and walk in the grace of Christ Jesus. Amen." He then leaned forward slightly and said to Kent, "You may kiss your bride."

Kent framed Odelia's beaming face with his hands, tilted his head and kissed her. And kissed her. She wrapped her hands around his wrists, and still he kissed her. Magnolia rolled her eyes, and Hypatia cleared her throat. Several of the guests began to chuckle. Petra laughed, tears streaming down her face.

Finally, Hubner muttered, "I believe that will do," at which point Kent at last raised his head.

"I have waited fifty years for that," he proclaimed loudly. "I meant to get fifty years of joy from it."

Odelia threw her arms around him with a happy cry, and the crowd erupted with teary laughter.

Hub spread his arms and announced, "It is my pleasure to present to you Mr. and Mrs. Kent Monroe."

Everyone in the room leapt to their feet and began to applaud. Kent looked as if he'd won the lottery, while Odelia gazed up at him adoringly.

As the happy couple left the room, Kent strutting as proudly as a peacock while Odelia clung to his arm and bounced with giggles, Dallas leaned forward far enough to catch her sister's eye. "Have you ever seen anyone so happy?"

"No," Petra admitted. "You were right about them."

Dallas gave Garth a strangely satisfied smile that alarmed Dale. Was Dallas promoting a match between her sister and Garth Anderton? Or did she consider the match already made? Had he read too much into Petra's intention to introduce him to her parents? Even if he hadn't misread her, he conceded silently, it was possible that things had changed since Garth's return to town. Dale had not one shred of doubt that Anderton had been doggedly, carefully grooming her to be his next conquest. He had assumed, however, that Petra was too smart and independent to fall for Anderton's charm.

A few moments later, the last of the wedding procession passed, and Dale stepped out into the aisle. He turned and moved back, making room for Petra to step out in front of him. Quickly crowding forward again, he made sure that Anderton could not squeeze in ahead of him and followed Petra up the packed aisle.

"Wasn't it beautiful?" she asked as they reached the vestibule, glancing back over her shoulder.

Not as beautiful as you, he thought, taking in her knee-length dress and spike heels. Before he could speak, however, Dallas was suddenly there, reminding her sister that they were to ride to the reception with their brother Phillip. Nodding, Petra turned to Dale.

Go with me, he started to say, anxious to have her to himself for a few minutes at least, but he only got the first word out before Dallas dragged Petra away, proclaiming that their mother wanted them back at Chatam House before everyone else. Dale watched them disappear into the throng, his spirits diving.

He made his way out of the building with agonizing slowness, then fought his way through the traffic to Chatam House. Guests packed the place by the time he got inside the building. The wedding gifts were being stored in the cloakroom, and he actually had to stand in line to get to the door. Once there, the uniformed girl who'd taken the gift asked for his name. She looked down a list before pointing to a diagram of the ballroom with circles drawn in to represent dining tables and triangles to represent chairs.

"You're at table number three, Mr. Bowen, Seat H."

He thanked the attendant and made his way down the east corridor to the first of two sets of wide open doors.

Music played softly. At first, he assumed it was a recording, until he turned his head and saw that the Chatam triplets had booked a small chamber orchestra for the occasion. The black-clad performers sat between two baby grand pianos arranged upon a small stage at one end of the room. A section of movable wall had been pushed back so they could be seen. Huge flower arrangements atop four-foot-tall columns flanked the stage. Similar arrangements stood along the walls and in the far corners. Every table in the room, at least two dozen, bore flowers, including the cake table, where a four-tiered cake dripping with sugar camellias and a large sheet cake entirely covered in pink sugar rosebuds, each with a strawberry at its center, sat on display.

The wedding party stood in a receiving line before a table placed near the wall between the doors to the room, with the laughing newlyweds at its center. Dale dutifully stood in line, inching closer as others made their best wishes known to the happy couple.

While he waited, he scanned the room for Petra. Failing to find her, he looked for table three instead. A few moments later, he shook hands with Kent and pressed a dry kiss to Odelia's plump cheek, then went to find his chair.

He sat alone at the table for some time, until Hubner

Chatam went to a microphone and spoke a blessing on the meal about to be served. An army of white-coated waiters with pink cummerbunds immediately brought out appetizers of shrimp cocktail. Finally, the others came—first Asher and Ellie, Kent's granddaughter, then Dallas and a very tall, slender, dark-haired fellow whom Dale remembered from the church. He introduced himself as, "Phillip Chatam, the other brother."

"What are you doing at this table?" Dallas demanded of Dale, frowning.

Taken aback, Dale spread his hands. "All I know is that the girl in the cloakroom told me this is my seat assignment."

Dallas turned a critical eye on the table. "Nine! That's going to be a squeeze."

"I suppose we'll just have to manage," said an all-too-familiar voice. Dale turned, greeting Anderton with a frown.

"I thought you were supposed to be in Colorado."

"On the contrary," Anderton said with a cheeky grin. "I wouldn't miss this special evening for anything."

Petra arrived with her parents just then. She seemed surprised to see Dale at the table, but quickly introduced him to Maryanne and Murdock Chatam before allowing him to seat her on his immediate left. To Dale's relief, Anderton found his place card across the table, next to Dallas.

Dale didn't much like that the Chatams seemed well acquainted with Garth, and he actively disliked the manner in which Garth said to Petra's parents, "Dale is the junior half of Bowen & Bowen Construction, the contractors on the hotel renovation."

"And he handled the renovation here at Chatam House, too," Dallas put in, adding meaningfully, "himself."

Dale refrained from so much as glancing in her direction, but he felt that dig sharply. His heart warmed when Petra came immediately to his defense.

"Dale is an excellent carpenter and an expert in antique building methods. In fact, he has a degree in archaeology."

"Not exactly," he corrected. "My degree is in history with an emphasis in archaeology. I decided against the advanced degree."

"And why is that?" Petra's mother asked.

"I thought about teaching, but I'm a hands-on kind of guy," Dale explained forthrightly, "which is why I considered archaeology, but then my father became ill, so I came home to help with the family business."

"And what is your father's diagnosis?" asked Murdock Chatam, the physician.

"Ventricular fibrillation brought on by physical exhaustion."

"I see. There are excellent treatments available now," Murdock said. "They ought to be able to manage his symptoms, provided he doesn't continue to overdo."

"Which is exactly why I'm here," Dale pointed out, "to take as much off him as I can."

"Dale hopes his father will retire once the hotel renovation is completed," Petra supplied.

"Is that likely?" Murdock asked.

"Maybe," Dale answered. Looking at Petra he added, "If we can secure the right help, I think he can be persuaded."

Dale knew the perfect person for the job. He was staring at her. He had in mind a very permanent position, one he had prayed about for many hours. He could only hope that she would eventually find the arrangement to her liking.

Chapter Fourteen

The second course arrived, a salad. Anderton attempted to monopolize the conversation by bragging on Petra.

"Speaking of the right help," he began, addressing Murdock and Maryanne, "you'll be happy to know that your daughter has done a smash-up job thus far." He went on to detail much of Petra's work, summing up with, "I have no doubt that she'll be an excellent manager once the Anderton Vail is open for business."

"I couldn't agree more," Dale put in, looking at Petra. "I think she's one of the best managers I've ever worked with."

She thanked him with a smile, prompting Anderton to proclaim, "She could wind up running my European acquisitions inside of a year."

"That's wonderful!" Maryanne Chatam exclaimed.

"Well done," Murdock congratulated. "I knew you'd hit your stride."

Petra merely nodded and looked at her lap. She didn't seem as pleased as she should have by the praise of her parents, but Dale realized he couldn't ask her about that while sitting at the table with them. He would try to find an opportunity to speak to her alone after the meal. At least sitting beside her allowed him some conversation. He managed to engage her with small talk from time to time through an entrée of filet mignon and grape potatoes with asparagus hollandaise, followed by a plate of fruit.

"The wedding was wonderful," he said.

"Very moving," Petra agreed, adding with a little laugh, "I cried so much I had to repair my makeup before I could show my face here."

"You look lovely," Garth immediately put in from across the table.

Dale had wanted to tell her the same thing, but Garth had beat him to it, so he said instead, "Don't women always cry at weddings?"

"A wedding fifty years in the making ought to evoke tears," Dallas interjected. "I remind you that I engineered the renewed romance which precipitated said wedding."

"Yes, we have all heard," her mother said with a touch of impatience.

"But you can't manufacture a romance out of thin air," Petra stated pointedly. "They were already in love."

"And had been for fifty years," Asher noted.

"A smaller wedding might have been more tasteful," Murdock murmured, glancing around the room, "given their ages."

"Oh, Aunt Odelia will never grow old," Phillip said with a chuckle. "I considered giving them a climb as a wedding gift."

That moved conversation into his line of work—mountain climbing.

"I'm not one of the main guides," he told Dale, "more of an operations manager, but I fill in when I'm needed."

His mother frowned at this. "You're too thin, Phillip, which tells me that you've been on that mountain more than you admit."

"I spend most of my time in an office, as you well know," Phillip said calmly.

"Still," Dale felt compelled to say, "it's dangerous work, isn't it?"

Phillip brushed that off. "Our company has teams on the highest peaks in the world, but we've never lost a climber, not a guide or a client."

"That's an impressive track record," Dale admitted, "and I enjoy a thrill as much as anyone, but I can just imagine what my parents would have said if I had decided on so risky an occupation. My mother already worries that I'll cut off a thumb or some such thing," he added with a chuckle.

"We try to respect the individuality of our children," Maryanne Chatam said stiffly. "Let them find their own way."

Dale glanced at Petra and found her frowning in contemplation.

"We aren't all intrigued by antique light fixtures and rooms without closets," Garth quipped. Dale smiled tautly at his napkin, just about fed up with these little digs.

Petra laid down her fork, saying starchily, "Excuse me while I visit the ladies' room." She glared at her sister. "Dallas, you can come with me."

Both Dale and Garth immediately came to their feet as the sisters pushed back their chairs, both frowning. Dale couldn't very well follow after the women, so he murmured something about needing to stretch his legs and made for the other set of doors, but no sooner did he step out into the hallway than he felt a hand latch on to his arm. He turned to find Garth Anderton smiling crookedly.

"Why don't you give it up, old boy. She's out of your league."

"I don't dispute it," Dale told him, lifting his chin, "but I'll 'give it up,' as you say, when she tells me to and not before."

"I offer her everything she's ever dreamed of," Garth pointed out, "a stellar career, world travel, wealth, status. I can give her an even better life than she's already known. What do you have to offer her?"

My heart, Dale thought, *children, a loving family, a job working right along beside me, if she likes, a common faith.* That seemed like enough—until Garth reached into his coat pocket and brought out a diamond ring the size of a walnut.

"I had planned to wait," he said, "but you've forced my hand."

Dale knew he would never be able to afford something like that. The best he could do was his great-grandmother's old wedding set, which he had inherited as the only grandson. The main diamond was nearly a full carat, but the others were just bits of sparkle in an old-fashioned gold setting. It held a wealth of sentimental value, however, and he'd always imagined how proud his mother would be when he slid those rings onto his bride's hand.

But could Petra be happy with that?

"I don't understand why you're not happy!" Dallas exclaimed, throwing up her hands as Petra closed the door to the family parlor off the back hallway. "Your career's on track, our parents are thrilled with you, and one of the world's most attractive men is in love with you!"

Petra gasped, her mood lightening instantly. "Do you think so?"

Dallas parked her hands at her waist. "You don't think he flew back here just to attend Aunt Odelia's wedding, do you?"

Oh, Petra thought, deflated. *Garth. Of course.*

Sighing, she put a hand to her head. "Garth falls in and out of love with the seasons."

"You don't know that," Dallas scoffed.

"He's already been married and divorced twice, Dallas."

"Maybe he finally met the right woman."

"And maybe he's fallen right back into a familiar pattern,"

Petra countered. "Both of his ex-wives were employees of Anderton Hotels."

Dallas frowned. "Maybe they went after him."

"Are you suggesting that Garth is attracted to me because I *haven't* gone after him?"

Folding her arms, Dallas plopped down on one of a pair of comfy flowered sofas. "Why haven't you?" she asked.

"I don't know," Petra admitted. "Maybe I was too focused on work. Or maybe he's just not the right man for me."

"You won't know unless you give him a chance," Dallas pleaded.

"It's too late for that," Petra told her, shaking her head.

Gasping, Dallas popped to her feet. "Has Dale Bowen asked you to marry him?"

"No."

"Good! Because Garth is the man for you. I know it."

"Dallas," Petra said, rolling her eyes, "you are not God's little matchmaker. Take care of your own love life, and let me take care of mine."

"I hadn't noticed you have one," Dallas muttered.

"Well, stay tuned," Petra told her smartly, heading for the door. "I just might surprise you."

Dallas gusted out a deep sigh. "Really, Petra," she snapped, "are you ready to be the kind of wife that Dale Bowen surely expects?"

Petra paused, half turning, to say, "I'm ready to be the kind of wife that God wills me to be." With that, she left her sister and went back to the reception.

Dale lounged near the stairwell until he saw Petra return to the ballroom through the doors at the far end of the hallway. He pushed away from the wall, intending to return to the table, only to draw back as Garth stepped into view. Clearly, the other man had been lying in wait for her in the hall on the other side of the staircase. Dallas joined him an instant later. Laying a hand upon his arm, she stretched up to speak softly into Garth's ear as he bent toward her. The two engaged in a quiet but spirited conversation. Then Garth checked his wristwatch and looked toward the ballroom. Dale swiftly took off, beating Garth to the table by mere steps.

Petra's cousins, Harmony and Lyric, had begun a spirited piano duet, using different pianos, while the orchestra took a break. The room was crowded with too many tables to allow any sort of dancing, so Dale opted for a stroll on the patio.

"Maybe you'd like to join me?" he asked Petra.

She immediately got to her feet again. "Of course."

Dale offered Petra his arm and took a small measure of comfort in the way she curled her own around it. They wound their way through the tables and out the glass doors at the end of the room to the patio beyond. Others were taking advantage of the terra-cotta-tiled outdoor space, which had been arranged with potted trees, hanging pots of flowers and glowing lanterns. Several guests sat on the ledge of the rectangular fountain, letting the breeze that blew across the water feature cool them.

"Ah," Petra said, "this feels good. I was a little chilled in the other room."

"Would you like my coat?" Dale asked, ready to shrug out of it.

Petra laughed. "No, thank you. It's quite warm out here."

"Well, it is Texas in June," Dale commented dryly.

"Yes, it is," she said, moving toward a corner of the expansive patio. "I'm glad we came out. I've been wanting to tell you something."

"Oh? What's that?"

She went to stand with her back to the white painted brick of the wall between two tall windows. Music from the room beyond filtered into the night.

"I've been thinking about some of the things you've said," she told him, "and you're right."

"That's nice," Dale quipped, smiling. "About what, exactly?"

"For one thing," she said, drawing her slender brows together thoughtfully, "I have held my family at bay somewhat. I didn't realize it until you told me I ought to reach out to them. I think I let resentments and insecurities from my childhood dictate my behavior."

"And I think it takes a wise, mature and caring woman to admit that," he praised, settling a hand at the nape of her neck.

She tilted her head, resting her cheek briefly against his arm. "I don't know about that. I do know that I want to be closer to my family. We may never be the Bowens, but we do care for each other."

"I can see that," he told her.

Smiling, she looked down and softly said, "You were also right that it isn't an either/or proposition when it comes to career and marriage."

Dale felt his heart *thunk* inside his chest. He wanted to gather her into his arms and hug her to his chest, but he managed to curtail that impulse by glancing around at the others on the patio. "What changed your mind?" he asked gently.

She lifted her gaze to his and eagerly queried, "Have you ever read the thirty-first chapter of Proverbs?"

Thinking swiftly, Dale recalled a particular verse. "'Charm is deceptive, and beauty is fleeting,'" he quoted, "'but a woman who fears the Lord is to be praised.'"

"'Honor her for all that her hands have done,'" Petra went on, "'and let her works bring her praise at the city gate.'"

"That passage seems to have made quite an impression on you," he observed, pleased.

"And the ones before it," she affirmed, growing animated. "They're all about the worthy wife."

He remembered another snippet. "A wife of noble character…is worth far more than rubies."

"And she conducts her own business. She manufactures goods, buys and sells, even land. The Bible explicitly says that she turns a profit."

"So she contributes to the household income," he surmised, nodding.

"It even talks about how she should treat her servants," Petra went on enthusiastically.

Servants, Dale mentally echoed, remembering suddenly what she'd said before about the "household staff." Garth's words from earlier ran through his mind. *"I can give her an even better life than she's already known."*

Dale gulped. He'd convinced himself that she had been alluding to marriage to him! More likely, she was just talking about marriage in general. Or possibly, marriage to Garth Anderton. Before he could even begin to sort that out, Maryanne Chatam appeared at his elbow, gesturing for Petra to return to the ballroom.

"Hurry," she urged. "You don't want to miss this."

Petra smiled and moved to her mother's side, linking arms with her. She gestured for Dale to join them, but his faltering steps left him trailing along behind. He had to wonder if that would not always be the case.

Kent towed a giggling Odelia to the microphone at the front of the stage as someone rolled in a bulletin board with its empty back to the room.

"Here it comes," Dale murmured, smiling wanly.

Petra shot him a surprised glance as Kent began to speak.

"A groom who has waited as long as I have for his bride naturally wants to give her an amazing wedding gift," he began.

He followed with an amusing story of taking Odelia to a swimming party in the early 1960s where he had wound up fully clothed in the pool. While he had soaked the seat of his '57 Chevy driving home, she had enthused about the possibility of having her own pool one day. Petra recalled that Odelia had said the same many times, but Grandpa Hub had always considered a private pool unnecessarily pretentious. After his death, Petra couldn't recall Odelia bringing up the matter again.

Kent finished his speech by addressing Odelia personally, saying, "So it is my hope, dear one, that this will fulfill one small dream for you."

With that, he made a twirling motion with one hand, and the attendant spun the board. Odelia gasped and began to hop up and down. "A pool! A pool!" she cried, turning the board so the whole room could see the artist's detailed rendering of what Kent intended to install in the backyard just on the other side of the patio.

Kent announced that Magnolia and Hypatia had kindly given their consent to have the pool built, and Odelia ran to them with hugs and kisses before trotting back to shower Kent with the same, while their guests laughed and clapped.

"You knew about this?" Murdock asked of Dale, and the latter nodded.

"He showed me the plans. I made a few suggestions concerning the cabana, so it would blend in better with the house."

Odelia waved her hankie for attention then and went to the microphone, saying, "This makes my gift look paltry, I'm afraid." She waved her hankie again, and two waiters rolled in the largest flat-screen TV Petra had ever seen. It required two dollies to move it.

"Good grief," Dallas exclaimed, "where on earth are they going to put that?"

"Not in their suite," Dale ventured. "I can't think of a single wall where it could be viewed from."

Odelia solved that mystery by thanking her sisters for

agreeing to have the television mounted in the family parlor.
Kent laughed and made much of the gigantic TV until the
waiters wheeled it out again. Then it was time to cut the cake.
After the appropriate pictures were taken, the cake went the
way of the television set and bulletin board. It began appearing again shortly in generous pieces of strawberry confec-
tion topped with creamy white frosting and sugar camellias,
alongside slivers of chocolate cake and confectioner's roses.
The waiters moved swiftly through the room, depositing dessert plates at every table setting.

Kent and Odelia, meanwhile, made their own way from
table to table, thanking their guests for attending. When they
reached table three, Odelia had yet another announcement
to make, specifically for Petra.

"That nice Mr. Anderton," she said, "has given us a wedding gift of five nights at any of his hotels. Which one would
you suggest we choose?"

Dallas smiled like a cat who'd trapped a canary in its
mouth. Ignoring her, Petra advised them to choose the
Mahila House in Hawaii or the Wallace in Boston. Obviously impressed, Kent and Odelia looked at each other and
beamed.

"I think we'll be having two honeymoons, my love," Kent
told her, chortling as they moved on to the next table.

"That was very generous of Garth," Dallas praised.

Petra sent her a pointed look and glanced around the table,
surprised to find Garth absent. "He can afford it."

Dallas went into a pout and didn't emerge again until it
came time to toss the garter. Kent put out a call for all single
men to gather at the front of the room.

Phillip looked around with a pained face. "That's me."

Dale shrugged and said, "Me, too."

Petra offered him a smile of encouragement as he and
Phillip rose and began reluctantly making their way to the
front of the room. She thought she'd made definite headway

out on the patio. He hadn't really said that he wouldn't mind a working wife, but he'd seemed to understand that there were no Scriptural strictures against it.

A cheer went up from the crowd at the front of the room then, and she fixed her attention there. After a moment, Dale strolled out of the crowd. He shrugged and held out his hands, showing that he'd come away empty-handed. Petra saw, to her consternation, that Garth brandished the lacy garter. Beaming, he slipped it on over the sleeve of his tuxedo coat. Dale walked back to his chair and sat down, a complacent look on his face that she couldn't interpret.

Phillip tried to fill the silence with a jocular quip. "Well, we were lucky this time."

Dale chuckled. "I don't believe in luck. I believe in God's will. Besides, Anderton was quite anxious to get his hands on that trinket."

"He was, wasn't he?" Phillip muttered.

"Let him have it," Dale said mildly.

Petra fought a surge of disappointment. It was just a silly garter, for pity's sake, but it seemed almost like an omen. Surely, if Dale was thinking about marriage, he'd have tried to catch the thing. She told herself that she was being foolish, but she hadn't realized just how far along the path of matrimony her feelings had taken her. In a little less than a month, she'd gone from single-minded focus on her career, despite Garth's attempts at securing her interest, to hoping that Dale Bowen would propose.

Odelia and Kent went off to change into traveling attire. The orchestra returned to play another set, and then it was time for the bouquet toss. Odelia herself came and got Petra. Dressed in pink silk crepe and the largest cameo earrings that Petra had ever seen, she still wore the ivory silk headband and sash, a cameo the size of a saucer pinning the latter in place. Petra couldn't help smiling when Odelia stuck her right in front of the other single women.

When the bouquet came sailing directly toward her, however, Petra stepped aside. If Dale wasn't to have the garter, then she wouldn't have the bouquet. The thing plopped right into Dallas's hands. Her sister's mouth fell open, and she dropped the bouquet as if it had bitten her. Bending, Petra swept up the thing, a smaller version of the one Odelia had actually carried at the church, and thrust it back into Dallas's grasp.

"Congratulations," she said pointedly and turned away.

She caught a glimpse of Garth's horrified face as he stared at Dallas with that bouquet in her hands. Petra laughed. She just couldn't resist.

Neither Dallas nor Garth returned to the table immediately. Instead, they were herded off to have photos taken. Then it was time for the bride and groom to leave amidst a hail of birdseed on the front lawn.

"Any idea where they're going?" Dale asked.

Before Petra could tell him that the newlyweds would spend the night in Waco then go on to San Antonio for a few days, someone's phone rang.

"Anderton," she heard Garth say. Then, "I see. We'll be right there."

The next thing she knew, Garth had seized her by the hand. "Lousy timing, I know," he said apologetically. "But we have to get down to the hotel. Something about an unscheduled delivery."

Petra frowned. "I can't imagine what it could be."

"Well, I certainly don't know," Garth said. "I've been out of town for most of the past three weeks. You'll have to come with me."

Petra sighed. "Oh, all right." At least the reception was over. She turned to Dale, who stood frowning behind her. "Sorry."

"Not a problem," he told her. "Are we still on for tomorrow?"

Breakfast. "Yes," she called as Garth dragged her away, "but I'll have to call you with the details."

Nodding, Dale waved. Petra offered him a last smile as Garth bundled her into the passenger seat of his rental car. Five minutes later, they pulled up to the curb in front of the hotel. Garth got out, so she followed suit.

"I don't see anyone trying to make a delivery," she said, just as a strange man opened the front door of the building and walked out. "Well, I never!" she exclaimed. "How did he get in?"

"I'll ask," Garth said, going over to the man. Something changed hands, then the fellow went on his way. Garth waved her over. "We'd better take a look inside."

He took her straight to the elevator. "What is this about?" she asked, but he just smiled and punched a button on the panel.

"You'll see." As the floors flowed past, she realized they were going to the penthouse.

"This isn't about work, is it?" she asked, both saddened and wary.

"It can be if you want it to be," he said as the elevator door slid open. "On the other hand," he went on, ushering her quickly forward, "you don't ever have to work another day in your life if you don't want to."

He threw open the door to the apartment. Soft music flowed from a room filled with roses and flickering candles. She saw by the light of a candelabra that the dining table had been set for two. It was the perfect romantic setting—and meant only cringing discomfort to her. A very different scene rose before her mind's eye—a picture of Dale sitting on a park bench in the sweltering heat, patiently patting a crying toddler.

Garth reached into his pocket and brought out a ridiculously large diamond set in a slender platinum band. She thought of Dale standing beneath the porte cochere at Chatam House last tonight.

"You look like a million bucks."

Her heart turned over. She didn't need a million bucks or a big diamond or even romance. She didn't even need a job. She just needed Dale.

Looking at Garth now, she felt so very sorry that she'd ignored all his overtures these past months. It would have been much better if she'd just walked away, but she had let ambition and insecurity dictate her actions. No longer. Never again.

Lifting a hand to Garth's cheek, she told him softly but firmly, "No."

He blinked at her. "But I haven't even asked—"

"Don't," she interrupted, shaking her head.

"Just hear me out," he argued.

"It won't change anything. I'm in love with someone else."

His lips flattened into a determined line. "That carpenter is not for you. Even your sister says so! I won't give up. Every day I'll—"

"Then I quit," Petra said calmly.

"Quit?" His eyes widened almost comically.

"I can't work with you anymore," she explained, backing away, "and I can't do this." She waved a hand at the room in which she had not even set foot. "I have to go now."

She hurried back to the elevator. As the doors slid closed on Garth's perplexed face, she thought he looked as confused as she had been.

"Okay, Lord, now what?" she asked as the elevator dropped.

Suddenly she was out of a job. Again. How was she going to support herself? Could she even manage to stay in town?

The aunties probably wouldn't object, but she couldn't live off them, and if she couldn't find some kind of job around here, then what about Dale?

Chapter Fifteen

Dale watched from his mom's sedan as Dallas pulled up behind Anderton's rental car. He was surprised he'd beat her here, but not at all amused that his instincts had been right. When he'd seen her slip her cell phone into her evening bag on the porch of Chatam House, he'd suspected that the urgent phone call Garth had received had come from her. Since she hadn't been around when Garth had literally dragged Petra away with him, Dale could only assume that Dallas knew where they were going because she had arranged to send them there.

He wondered what plan she had concocted, and if Anderton was a part of it. When Petra burst out of the building, he thought he was about to get his answer. He rolled down the window in time to hear Dallas demand, "Well?"

"I knew you had something to do with this!" Petra accused.

"Never mind about that," Dallas complained. "Did he ask you?"

Petra dropped her hands onto her hips, striking a pose. "You mean, did Garth propose marriage to me?"

Dale's heart dropped into his stomach.

"Of course I mean that!" Dallas snapped.

"No," Petra said firmly. "He did not."

"What? But he had the whole thing arranged, a grand gesture that no woman in her right mind wouldn't find romantic!"

"He didn't ask," Petra reiterated, "and it's a good thing, because I'd have had to turn him down. In addition to quitting my job."

Such relief swamped Dale that he almost missed Dallas's scoffing laugh. "As if you'd do such a thing."

"But I did do such a thing," Petra said. "It isn't the first time I've quit a job, you know."

Petra had quit her job? Dale's jaw descended.

"But...this is your big chance!" Dallas pointed out. "You've said it over and over again."

"I was wrong," Petra told her, going to the passenger side of Dallas's car and opening the door. "God willing, I have a chance at something bigger than any career, Dallas. I only hope it works out the way I want it to. Now take me home." With that, she got into the car.

Throwing up her hands, Dallas stomped around to get behind the wheel. Moments later, they drove away.

Dale sat where he was, thinking. Was he the chance of which Petra had spoken? Would she give up her job, her vaunted career, for *him?*

"Not if I can help it," he muttered. All he wanted was for her to be happy, and he was beginning to believe he could make that happen. "Please, Lord," he whispered.

Suddenly the thought occurred to him that he needed to make a grand gesture of his own, something unique to him, something Anderton would never dream of, something truly meaningful and audacious. He'd made a fool of himself for far lesser reasons, but what would convince Petra—and everyone else—that she belonged with him?

He would think on it, he decided, and pray on it, and

something would come to him, something that would make everyone see that, to him, she was the most important thing in this world.

Alone in her room an hour or so later, Petra sat down on the sofa and took her Bible in her hands. She had told her parents only that she had quit her job. If they knew why, then Dallas had told them, but none of that really mattered to Petra. She knew she ought to be worried. Not only did she have no job, she had no real reason to hope that Dale was even considering marriage to her. Still, she felt an odd peace. For once, she knew what she truly wanted.

Petra opened her Bible to the thirty-first chapter of Proverbs and, closing her eyes, laid her hands flat upon the page. Then she began to pray.

"I've been confused and wandering for a long time," she told God, "but I know now that I want to be this woman. I want to be this woman for Dale, but he has to want me for that, too, and so do You. I know that if You will it, Lord, it must surely be. So I'm asking You now, please, please help me be the kind of wife…and mother…who is worth more than rubies. Help me be what I never thought I could be, what I judged my own mother of failing to be. And forgive me, Lord, for holding on to petty grievances and letting them rule my life."

Lapsing into silence, she went on for a long while, pouring out her every fear, question, resentment, praise, speculation and hope, placing each and every one into the Father's keeping.

By the time Petra laid down her head that night, her eyes felt gritty with fatigue and her mind had gone blank, but she had found a measure of peace. That would do for now. She would worry about tomorrow when tomorrow came, trusting her Lord to see her through whatever would be.

* * *

Petra slept well, resting deeply. Awaking before her alarm went off, she stretched and rose to quickly sweep her hair up into a ponytail and dress for the day in a sunny yellow tank top and pink denim capris, with a short matching jacket. She chose the tank top simply so she could wear her yellow sequined flip-flops with the outfit. They made her smile, and she felt like smiling today. She was determined to, in fact.

Only as Petra took a seat at the table in the sunroom with her parents and brother Phillip did she recall that she'd invited Dale to join them for breakfast then hadn't followed through with the arrangements! Gasping, she pulled out her cell phone and began going through her contacts for Dale's number. When the call connected, she knew at once that she'd been diverted to his voice mail.

"Hi!" Dale's voice said brightly. "Dale Bowen here. I can't talk now, but your call's important to me, so I'll get back to you as soon as I can. You know what to do next. Thanks."

Petra waited for the beep then began apologizing. "I'm so sorry! I forgot to tell you what time to come for breakfast. If you get this message within the next half hour, please come by Chatam House. I mean, i-if you want to and you can. Mom and Dad are leaving in a little while, and…okay, if you can't come by, maybe you could just…call me?"

Her phone beeped before she got the last word all the way out, letting her know that another call was coming in. Sure that it must be Dale, she didn't even bother checking the caller ID, just punched the green icon and put the phone back to her ear.

"Hello?"

"You need to get down here, Petra!" exclaimed Garth's agitated voice.

Disappointed, Petra fell back in her chair and folded an arm across her chest as she said, "I don't work for you any-~ore, remember?"

"I haven't seen a letter of resignation yet!" Anderton barked.

"I'll email one today," she promised.

"Fine. Whatever. But that's beside the point. Your crazy boyfriend is sabotaging everything!"

Petra sat up straight again. "What do you mean?" He couldn't mean *Dale*. Dale was the last person to sabotage anything.

"I mean, that loony carpenter is going to get himself arrested if you don't get down here and put a stop to this insanity!"

He did mean Dale! But why… How…? Those questions obviously would have to wait. Though it boggled the mind, if Dale was in danger of being arrested, then she had to get down there.

She hopped to her feet, crying, "I'm on my way!"

"What on earth?" her mother demanded, also rising.

"Where are you going?" her father asked, pushing back his chair.

"To the hotel!" she told them, weaving her way through the jungle of bamboo furniture.

She met Hypatia in the hallway, and her urgency must have communicated itself clearly, for her dear auntie threw up a hand.

"Petra! What's wrong?"

"I don't know," she answered, sliding past her aunt and breaking into a run, "but Dale's in trouble! Garth says he could be arrested!"

Dashing up the stairs, she grabbed her handbag and jacket and flew back down to the ground floor again. As she raced across the foyer, she heard Hypatia say, presumably to Chester, "Bring the car around while I phone Asher."

Then Petra threw open the front door and ran for her car, all the while scrabbling for her keys. She managed to get her hand on the remote and unlock the driver's door before she got there. Yanking it open, she tossed the handbag onto the passenger seat and dove inside. Thirty seconds later, the low-slung coupe turned onto the street and laid down some rubber.

She had no idea what was going on, but she prayed fervently that Dale would come to no harm. Garth's words still made no sense to her, and she couldn't imagine what to expect. But it certainly was not what she found.

There seemed to be a traffic jam of some sort at the north corner of the downtown square. Some vehicles, in fact, executed tricky U-turns or turned suddenly onto side streets. People milled around among the cars and pickup trucks, looking to the south. Desperate to get through, Petra grabbed the first available parking space and struck out on foot.

Dodging pedestrians right and left, she made her way down the east side of the square all the way to the corner and Monroe's Modern Pharmacy and Old-Fashioned Soda Fountain, Kent's drugstore, which was run mostly by his young partner now. There she encountered a policeman setting up a barrier of painted sawhorses.

"Stand back!" he ordered. "Everyone back!"

Petra rushed forward instead, her heart pounding, and began to plead with him. "I've got to get through! I'm Petra Cha—"

"Well!" he interrupted, grabbing her by the arm and practically dragging her around the end of the barrier. "You'd better see what you can do then." He pointed her in the direction of a police cruiser parked diagonally in the southeast intersection of the square, calling out, "Captain, this is Petra!"

Another policeman, this one with a bullhorn in hand, turned to wave her over, frowning. "Can you put a stop to this?" he asked sternly.

"I don't even know what's going on!"

He pointed a finger toward the hotel on the southeast

corner. At first, Petra saw only Garth standing on the sidewalk in his shirtsleeves, his phone to his ear, then someone on the corner opposite diagonally waved, and she looked in that direction. The entire Bowen family stood behind another police barricade erected there. Walt and Hallie waved madly, grinning. Behind them stood Jackie Hernandez and what looked like the whole Bowen and Bowen crew. Hallie, Petra noticed, carried a camera on a strap around her neck, and she aimed it at Petra now, snapping photos. To Hallie's left, Don hoisted Nell up onto his shoulder, as if they'd come to watch a parade! Completely confused, Petra shook her head at Sudie, who stood next to her husband and held little Callie on one hip. Dale's sister pointed upward insistently, jabbing a finger in the air.

Petra executed a slow turn, lifting her gaze as she did so. There hung a man in a harness from the edge of the roof of the hotel, five stories up. Her eyes widened as she recognized that man. Dale.

He faced away from her and held something in his hand. As she watched, his arm moved, and bright yellow paint sprayed in arcs over the dark red brick of the building. Petra gasped, unable to believe that Dale Bowen would deface any building, but especially a historic one, in such a fashion. Then her brain began to register what her eyes were seeing. He'd painted a message all along one side of the building, even across the upper windows.

"Petra," it read, "I love you!"

She nearly fell down, the rest of the words blurring as those first few sank in. Suddenly, Hypatia and Magnolia were at her elbow. Maryanne and Murdock arrived right behind them, her father exclaiming, "Good grief!"

To Petra's astonishment, her mother burst into tears. "Oh, my!" she wailed. "Will you just look at that? Isn't it wonderful?"

Petra felt her jaw drop just as the police captain chuckled

and folded his arms, the bullhorn still clasped in one hand. "Well?" he asked, cutting her an amused glance and nodding at the building. "What do you say?"

She looked upward again just in time to watch Dale put the finishing touch on a question mark, which came at the end of the sentence, "Will you marry me?"

Petra clacked her jaws shut again, but then she began to laugh, weak with astonishment and relief. Dale twisted around, pushing off from the building with one foot and wrapping his arm around the downspout of a gutter to hold himself in place. His gaze raked across the scene below and came to rest on her. He cupped his hands around his mouth and yelled, "I'm not coming down until you say yes!"

Still laughing, Petra grabbed the bullhorn out of the policeman's hand and found the trigger that operated it. As she did so, she saw Garth drop his hand, removing his phone from his ear. She shrugged, letting him know he'd been upstaged, grandly, and lifted the bullhorn to her face, pointing it toward Dale.

"I love you, too!" she shouted around the widest smile imaginable. "And yes, I will marry you!"

Everyone around her started talking at once, it seemed. She even heard cheering, but all her attention focused on Dale as he gave her a big double thumbs-up, put back his head and laughed. Someone took the megaphone out of her hand, but she hardly noticed because Dale chose that moment to let go of the downspout. He twisted around then reached up, released a catch on the line that held him above the ground and began rappelling down the face of the building.

Garth walked out into the intersection to watch. Petra laughed, tears running down her face as her loony carpenter, magnificent fiancé carefully placed his feet so that no windows were broken or bricks dislodged. When he hit the ground, he began unbuckling the harness. She moved toward him, but a hand fell on her shoulder. She turned reluctantly to find her parents there.

"Pet," her father said in a choked voice, "are you sure? A grand gesture like this can—"

"She's sure," said another voice. Dallas pushed forward, her eyes filled with tears. "If she was going to fall for a grand gesture, she already would have." Petra smiled and reached out a hand to her sister, who quickly squeezed her fingers and said, "Guess I was wrong this time." She seemed genuinely puzzled about that. "Go get him. He's waiting for you."

To Petra's everlasting surprise, Maryanne stepped up then and hugged her, whispering, "Be as happy as I have been."

"Thank you, Mom," Petra said sincerely. Then she tore away and ran to meet Dale.

Grinning, he stepped off the sidewalk, handing Garth a spray can as he passed by the other man. Garth motioned to the police captain, and for an instant Petra feared that Dale really would be arrested. She hoped Hypatia had been able to reach Asher! Glancing at the can, however, Garth held up a hand, not that any of the policemen had moved.

"Water solvent!" Garth announced loudly. He pointed the can at Dale's back, yelling, "And you're going to wash it off, too, Bowen!"

"I'll get right on that!" Dale retorted, opening his arms to Petra.

She flew into them, literally leaping at him. Catching her, he spun her around before setting her down again.

"Once I figured out what Anderton had been up to," he explained, "I figured I needed something dramatic to convince everyone that I'm the one you belong with."

"I was convinced a while ago," she told him, turning her gaze on the building again, "but it's a proposal no one's going to forget!"

"Your mountain-climbing brother gave me the idea," he

said, grinning. Then he cupped her face in his hands, low-ered his head and did his best Kent imitation.

Petra put her arms around as much of him as she could reach and kissed him back with every fiber of her being. Someone began to clap. Shortly, the whole square rang with applause. Dale dropped his arms around her and broke the kiss, motioning to his family. The Bowens trooped over, all talking at once.

"I knew she'd say yes."

"Who wouldn't say yes to my brother?"

"Oh, I'm so happy!"

"We're going to have another wedding, Mother. Our boy's getting married!"

After hugs all around and chatter that Petra didn't even try to follow, Dale held out his hand to his mother. She reached into a pocket and brought out a small bundle of tissue, which she carefully peeled away. As she turned over the contents of her hand into Dale's palm, she said, "These belonged to my grandmother. They were always meant for Dale's bride."

He picked up one ring and held it up for Petra to see. A nice emerald-cut diamond sat in the middle of a gold fili-gree band encrusted with smaller stones. "It's not much," he began, "and it's old-fashioned, so if you don't like it, we can—"

Petra snatched it out of his hand, lest he think he could alter that precious piece of jewelry in any way. "Don't you dare!" she exclaimed. "It's perfect!"

"Okay, okay," he laughed, taking it back and sliding it onto her finger. "We won't touch it." Petra closed her fist around it. "Well, maybe we'll have it sized so it won't fall off," he amended. "This one, too, I guess." He showed her the matching wedding band. Also filigree with tiny di-amonds tucked into every nook and cranny, it took her breath away.

"I've never seen anything like it."

"And you won't, either," Dale told her. "My great-grand-father had this made special."

"Over a hundred years ago," Hallie added.

"In Boston," Walt put in, as if that was significant some-how. And, funny enough, it was. Everything about this moment was.

Tears flowed from Petra's beautiful, warm-honey eyes.

"Oh, sweetheart, don't cry," Dale pleaded, taking her in his arms again. He couldn't bear the sight of her tears, even happy ones.

"Save the tears for the wedding," advised Petra's father from behind her.

Dale stiffened as Petra turned within the safe confines of his arms to face Murdock Chatam. Glancing around, Dale saw that the larger crowd was dispersing. Even now, the police were taking down the barricades and traffic was start-ing to move.

"I think we should step to the sidewalk," Murdock ad-vised, motioning to the corner in front of the pharmacy where Petra's family waited. Asher and Ellie stood beside Phillip, who had arrived with the Chatam sisters and Petra's parents. Dallas had shown up on her own early on, alerted, no doubt, by Garth Anderton. She hung back now, quite sub-dued.

Dale wrapped his arm around Petra just in case anyone thought she would be going anywhere without him for a while. She looped her arm around his waist to let him know that she was of the same mind, so he dropped another quick kiss on her sweet lips.

His family had been so certain that this would work, but Dale had had his doubts. The further he'd gotten into the thing, though, the more he'd believed. He'd taken a chance, risking everything, even his dad's health, when it came right down to it. But it had all been worth it.

As soon as they all congregated on the corner, Ellie opened the door to her grandfather's shop. "Let's go in here and get a cold drink."

They trooped into the pharmacy and over to the red-and-chrome counter. Magnolia and Hypatia moved to one of the booths at the end. Dallas and Phillip joined them, while Ellie went behind the counter to help Millie, the ancient clerk, draw and pass out glasses of ice water. Dale's family commandeered the other booth.

"Now then," Murdock said, standing behind his wife, who had taken one of the stools at the counter. "The wedding will be in Waco, of course."

"No, Dad," Petra contradicted him, slipping onto the stool next to her mom. "We're getting married here. Our family is here. Well, most of them. And all of Dale's."

"And Chatam House is here, too," Hypatia put in.

A phone rang. Dallas got up and moved away, digging in her pocketbook. Everyone ignored her.

Petra glanced at Dale and said, "Oh, I wouldn't want to put Hilda through another wedding so soon."

"Nonsense," Maryanne said. "It will be months, surely. A year, at least, if we have to manage the arrangements from Waco."

"No, ma'am," Dale told the woman gently, looking down at Petra. "Weeks, maybe, but not months."

"Days would be all right with me," Petra put in, eyes sparkling.

He grinned and dropped down onto the stool beside her. "I've got a good suit that's hardly seen any use."

"I can buy a dress in an hour."

"You have to wait until Odelia gets back from her honeymoon!" Magnolia spoke up. "It's bad enough that she missed the proposal."

Everyone laughed, and Phillip held up his phone, announcing, "I've got it on video."

"Me, too!" Hallie cried.

Dallas strolled up then and held out her phone to Petra. "Here. You'd better take this."

"Who is it?"

"Garth."

Dale pushed out a harsh breath. What now?

"He probably wants to fire me again."

"It's not like that," Dallas said. "He realizes...we *both* realize that you and Dale belong together. Besides," she added with a wry smile, "he has a hotel to finish. Just talk to him."

Petra looked to Dale. He reluctantly nodded. She took the phone in hand and pressed it to her ear. "Hello." A few minutes later, she lowered the phone again. "He says he'll pay for the honeymoon."

"What?"

"If we'll wait until after the hotel renovation is done," she hurried on, grinning.

"You mean, he's not canceling our contract?"

She shook her head. "He even wants to know if I'll come back and see the project through."

Flabbergasted, Dale couldn't think for a moment, but then he glanced at his dad and remembered what they'd talked about earlier. Spinning on the stool, he hung his elbows on the edge of the counter. "Fine by me," he decided, "if that's what you want. But from the Bowen & Bowen end of things."

Petra's brows lowered in confusion. "What do you mean?"

"We talked it over," Dale told her, "and we need you in the company. You've got the business savvy that I don't, and the organizational skills that neither Dad nor I have. Plus, I've worked with you enough to trust your judgment. Can't say the pay would be all that great, not at first anyway, but if you think about it, the benefits are special."

"Especially when the babies start coming," Hallie put in.

"That's right," Sudie said. "Mom and I will always be available to sit for you."

"Put a nursery in the office," Maryanne recommended. "That's what I did when my babies were small."

"You did?" Petra gasped, suddenly throwing her arms around her mother's neck. "I didn't know that!"

"Sounds like a great idea," Dale said eagerly.

Then he took the phone out of Petra's hand and put it to his own ear. "Did you get all that, Anderton?"

"I got it," the other man growled.

"Are we agreed?"

"Agreed," Anderton grumbled. "But I'll pay Petra's salary until this job is finished. And I expect it done on time and budget!"

"You have my word on it."

"That's good enough for me," Anderton said with a sigh.

"You know," Dale told him sincerely, "you're not half the jerk I thought you were."

"Why, thank you," came the acidic reply. "I am all aquiver with delight."

Dale laughed. "Just don't expect an invitation to the wedding." He ended the call without waiting for a reply and handed the phone back to Dallas. Looking at Petra, he said, "If it's all right with you, I'd as soon keep it pretty much family."

"Is that what you want, Petra?" Murdock asked. "A small, family-only wedding?"

"Just the immediate family, I think," she answered firmly, "and then later, after the job is finished, maybe a reception for everyone else. What do you think, hon?"

Dale grinned. "I think I like it when you call me 'hon,' so wedding now and reception later is fine with me."

"Okay," she said, lifting a hand to his cheek, "so how's Saturday?"

"Three days away!" her mother cried.

"Saturday it is," Dale agreed, turning his head to press a kiss into her palm. Now that was what he called answered prayer!

Epilogue

Petra and Dale were married in the front parlor at Chatam House at five o'clock in the evening. Odelia and Kent rushed back from San Antonio to get there in time. Phillip extended his stay in Texas, pleased to be able to make two weddings in one trip. Naturally, Hub presided. Garrett stood up with Dale, and Dallas with Petra, tears flowing the whole time. She still couldn't figure out how she'd been so wrong about Petra and Garth, but Hypatia had her own private suspicions about that.

Petra had found a lovely tea-length dress at a shop in Dallas where Hypatia had arranged a private viewing, and Jessa managed to put together some beautiful flowers, all yellows and pinks. Hilda, of course, insisted on baking a small cake, which she decorated with pink and yellow roses. Hallie provided Buttercup Punch, and agreed to share the recipe, which pleased Hilda to no end.

The rings had caused some consternation. Due to the age and value of the rings, the jeweler to which Asher had sent the newly engaged couple had not wanted to remove gold from the wedding set in order to cut down the size. Instead, he had recommended building up the rings from the inside at the top. As a wedding gift, Asher had offered to pay for the extra gold and filigree work. The result was very unique and pleasing, but Asher didn't arrive with the finished rings until an hour before the ceremony, and Petra didn't relax until that engagement ring was again on her finger.

After a small celebration, the happy couple went to spend the night at Garth Anderton's penthouse apartment in the hotel, Garth having left town. They would reside in Dale's apartment in the Bowen house for the time being and begin work on their own home sometime in the winter, after their delayed honeymoon. Hawaii seemed to be the leading contender for that trip.

With the house calm again and everyone seeking their beds, Hypatia traded her pearls and suit for ivory silk pajamas piped in navy and brushed out her hair. It had grown long of late, due to inattention, and needed a good cut. She would make an appointment with her hairdresser tomorrow. Too tired to even tie back her hair tonight, she padded out into the sitting room that she and Magnolia had shared alone the past three evenings.

Wearing flannel despite the summertime heat, dear old Mags sat in her usual spot at the end of the sofa, pensively unraveling her braid. She looked up when Hypatia came in and smiled.

"Sometimes I think we should hang a shingle."

"Whatever for, dear?"

"Wedding consultants."

Hypatia chuckled. "We've certainly had ample experience lately, haven't we?"

"I wonder who will be next," Magnolia mused.

"Bite your tongue!" Hypatia told her. "I, for one, could use a rest."

"Me, too," Odelia said, swanning into the room in a cloud of lilac chiffon and perfume.

Magnolia put both hands over her ears, exclaiming, "I don't want to know!"

"Well, I will tell you, anyway," Odelia cried in a huff, plopping down on the other end of the couch. "My husband snores." She giggled and added, "But only when he's exhausted."

Magnolia dropped her hands and rolled her eyes.

"Oh, it's all so romantic," Odelia sighed, hunching her shoulders. She went into a pout then, adding, "I wish I'd been there to see Dale's proposal."

"You've seen the video," Hypatia pointed out.

"Repeatedly," Magnolia muttered.

"I know, but it's not the same as being in the moment," Odelia said dreamily.

Hypatia smiled to herself. Not so much had changed, after all. Still, a new era had begun at Chatam House. Watching Magnolia with Garrett and his family tonight, seeing Hunter run around the place with Dale's two nieces, noting the way Odelia gazed so warmly at her husband and sensing the sizzling joy of Petra and Dale, Hypatia had felt great joy.

"Isn't life good?" she said suddenly, as surprised as her sisters.

"It's wonderful!" Odelia purred, lifting her shoulders and stretching out her legs to point her toes.

Magnolia seemed to ponder for a moment, but then she swallowed and Hypatia saw that she was fighting tears. "What is it, dear?" she asked, leaning forward.

Magnolia smiled, her eyes shining, and whispered, "Hunter asked if he could call me Grandma tonight. We settled on Grammy Mags."

"I'll tell you a secret," Odelia tittered, sliding to the edge of her seat. "I think I'm going to be a great-grandma before long."

"Ellie's pregnant?" Magnolia gasped.

"Soon."

Hypatia took a deep breath. Oh, yes, life was very good. "Well, then," she said, "in addition to praying God's blessings on the newest newlyweds tonight, we shall also pray that He reward her efforts."

As she reached out a hand toward each of her sisters, she marveled at all that God had wrought here at Chatam House. *And if life here in this old world can be so grand,* she told herself, *imagine what heaven must be like!* It would put the ceiling in the foyer of Chatam House to shame.

Or maybe not.

God's spirit had ever dwelled in this place, carried in the hearts of so many of His children. No wonder that love was so easily born here.

"May it ever be," Hypatia whispered. "May it ever be."

Leaning against the fender of his pickup truck, Dale sighed with satisfaction and tightened his arms about Petra's shoulders. She laid her head back against his shoulder, smiled and lifted her hands to his forearms, which were stacked loosely beneath her chin. Above the dark form of the magnolia tree in the side yard of Chatam House, the moon hung in the night sky, a perfect melon slice against velvet black. They had turned off the electric light of the porte cochere in order to see the starlight more clearly.

"Do you ever wonder what heaven is like?" Dale asked.

"Oh, yes."

"It must be like this," he mused in a husky voice.

Petra chuckled. "Maybe a little cooler than summer in Texas."

He smiled down at her. "Okay, I'll give you that. Otherwise, this evening is as perfect as you."

Frowning, Petra turned within the circle of his arms. "I'm nowhere near perfect. In fact, I have to tell you that, as happy as I am, I'm a little frightened, too."

Dale drew back a little, obviously troubled. "Frightened? Surely not of me."

She hooked her hands over the strong ridges of his shoulders. "No, of me. I want to be your wife and the mother of your children, but…"

"You want to work, too. I understand that and honor it."

"I—I'm just afraid that I won't be able to do it all," she confessed.

"Well, of course you can't," he said lightly, "not on your own. No one can. But you won't be alone in this. I'll be right here with you every step of the way. Together, with faith, we'll seek God's will at every turn, and He will never fail us."

* * * * *

Dear Reader,

I have been blessed to work from my home. This has been a joy and a blessing for me and my family, especially as so many moms do not have that luxury. Many wives and mothers work outside of their homes simply because they must. Let's face it, even those wives and mothers who do not work at "outside" occupations have full-time jobs just keeping their families going. So why would any wife and mother choose to work at a paying job outside of her home, let alone embark upon a career?

Well, because she can and, often, because she should.

Women have so much to offer! The man who understands this fact is wise, and the woman who finds such a man is blessed. As a careful study of Proverbs 31 shows, it has always been so, despite what some would have you believe. Hallelujah!

God bless,

Arlene James

Questions for Discussion

1. Petra's parents wanted their daughters to be career women, to "give back to society" and "make a difference in the world." Is this normal? Admirable?

2. Petra was confused about what her role should be. Should she marry or should she have a career? Do young women really struggle with this question?

3. Does conflict remain within the Christian community about a married woman's role and whether she should work outside her home? Why or why not?

4. For much of history, a woman's role was confined to the home. Did good reasons for that exist? If so, what were those reasons? Were some of those reasons unfair? If so, how and why?

5. Why would a wife and mother choose to work outside her home today?

6. Might the family of a woman who chooses to work outside her home suffer because of her decision? If so, how?

7. How can a woman who chooses to work outside her home keep her family from suffering because of her decision?

8. Dale's mother and sister both chose *not* to work outside the home. Why would a wife and mother choose *not* to work outside her home today?

9. Might the family of a woman who chooses *not* to work outside her home suffer because of her decision? If so, how?

10. How can a woman who chooses *not* to work outside her home keep her family from suffering because of her decision?

11. Proverbs 31:10-32 describes the "Wife of Noble Character." Can this description be applied to today's woman? Please detail.

12. As a parent, would you be supportive of an adult, married daughter who chose to work outside her home? Of an adult married daughter who chose *not* to work outside her home?

13. As a parent, would you be supportive of an adult, married daughter, *who is also a mother,* choosing to work outside her home? Of an adult married daughter, *who is also a mother,* choosing *not* to work outside her home?

14. Odelia Chatam and Kent Monroe chose to marry in their mid-seventies, well past the age when they might start a family. Why would they choose to do this? Does it seem reasonable to you? Why or why not?

15. Not only did Odelia and Kent choose to marry, they chose to do so in a certain style. What do you think of that choice? Does it seem reasonable to you? Why or why not?

INSPIRATIONAL

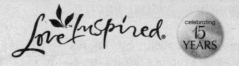

Love Inspired

celebrating 15 YEARS

COMING NEXT MONTH
AVAILABLE MAY 29, 2012

THE PROMISE OF HOME
Mirror Lake
Kathryn Springer

A DREAM OF HIS OWN
Dreams Come True
Gail Gaymer Martin

HEALING THE DOCTOR'S HEART
Home to Hartley Creek
Carolyne Aarsen

THE NANNY'S TWIN BLESSINGS
Email Order Brides
Deb Kastner

THE FOREST RANGER'S CHILD
Leigh Bale

ALASKAN HEARTS
Teri Wilson

REQUEST YOUR FREE BOOKS!

2 FREE INSPIRATIONAL NOVELS
PLUS 2
FREE
MYSTERY GIFTS

LIREG11B

celebrating 15 YEARS

Love Inspired

Get swept away with author

Carolyne Aarsen

Saving lives is what E.R. nurse Shannon Deacon excels at. It also distracts her from painful romantic memories and the fact that her ex-fiancé's brother, Dr. Ben Brouwer, just moved in next door. She doesn't want anything to do with him, but Ben is also hurting from a failed marriage...and two determined matchmakers think Ben and Shannon can help each other heal. Will they take a second chance at love?

Healing the Doctor's Heart

Home to
Hartley Creek

Available June 2012 wherever books are sold.

*The oldest Fitzgerald sibling, Ryan, is on the case tracking
down a killer, but will the victim's reporter cousin
Meghan Henry get in his way?*

*Read on for a sneak preview of
THE DEPUTY'S DUTY by Terri Reed,
the final book in Love Inspired® Suspense's exciting
FITZGERALD BAY miniseries.*

"The house is the second one on the right."

Deputy Chief Ryan Fitzgerald nodded to the officer
sitting next to him and tightened his grip on the steering
wheel. He pulled to the curb in front of a boxy house with
a front brick facade and white siding. The paved driveway
stood empty. He doubted this trip to the town of Revere
would pay off, but it was the only lead he had to a murder
suspect and a missing eighteen-month-old little girl.

He glanced around, taking stock of the neighborhood.
No one was out and about on this blistering June day.

His gaze snagged on a burgundy Subaru parked across
the street. His gut clenched.

Meghan Henry's car!

What was the nosy reporter doing here? Ever since
she'd arrived in Fitzgerald Bay six months ago she'd been
hounding him for answers in her cousin Olivia Henry's
murder. He didn't blame her for wanting to see justice done.
Olivia's death had rocked the community of Fitzgerald Bay
and the Fitzgerald family. She'd been Charles Fitzgerald's
nanny for his twins at the time of her death. Everyone
who knew her said she was a sweet woman. No one could
understand why someone would kill her.

So yes, Ryan understood Meghan's desire to see the
culprit arrested and put away, but not at the expense of
his family.

With everyone in town believing his younger brother, Charles, capable of killing Olivia Henry, all of the Fitzgerald Bay police force had worked overtime to clear his name. Meghan Henry's constant questions and snooping had hindered the investigation and inflamed the citizens of Fitzgerald Bay with suspicion.

And now here she was, poking around at the one lead he had to go on in another recent murder case.

Ryan was going to arrest Meghan for obstructing justice the second he saw her. He could imagine her wrinkling up her pert nose and daring him with her green-hued hazel eyes. The woman possessed a fiery spirit, for sure. A testament to her Irish heritage.

Pick up THE DEPUTY'S DUTY
to find out if Ryan and Meghan can work together to bring
peace to the town of Fitzgerald Bay once and for all.